# DARK
# ANGEL

A gripping crime thriller full of twists

## HELEN H. DURRANT

JOFFE
BOOKS

Published 2018 by Joffe Books, London.

www.joffebooks.com

ISBN- 978-1-912106-33-2

For my brother Christopher, his lovely wife Susan, and my nephew Tom.

# Prologue

Five months ago

Megan Farley hated music festivals. They were Leon's thing, not hers. She'd only come to this one because Leon promised to respray her car if she did. It was a mistake. The noise, the constant shrieking, even the music were all doing her head in. It never stopped, making sleep impossible. It had been three days without sleep, proper washing facilities or decent food.

They were in the depths of the beautiful Cheshire countryside, but the view was nothing but a sea of tents. The ground underfoot was a quagmire. It had rained hard since day one, so all the grass had been trampled to nothing.

She'd had enough. It was time to go. Leon would be angry. He'd keep on about how she was no fun, and tell her they were through. But Megan knew that once they were home, back into the routine of university life, he'd come round.

Leon and the others were off getting more booze. Giving one last backwards glance at the mayhem going on all around, Megan put the rucksack on her back and made for the field where her car was parked. It was quite a walk and the sun had gone down. She'd text Leon later. For now, it would take all her concentration to find her car in the dark.

Megan had gone no distance when she heard him calling her.

"Meggy? What's happened? Where are you off to?"

She'd hoped to be well on her way before he returned. "I'm off home," she called back. "I can't stand this any longer."

"The main act is on tonight. You said you liked them. Stay," he shouted. "One more night, then we'll both go back tomoz."

He didn't mean it. Come tomorrow there'd be another reason to stay. Megan knew very well that Leon wouldn't leave until the final number had been played.

"I've had enough," she shouted back. "You stay if you must, but I can't take any more. The food is gross, the noise unbearable, and as for the toilet block . . ." She pulled a face and shook her head.

"You're a selfish bitch, Meggy. You promised you wouldn't do this."

Megan heard him slam the crate of beers onto the ground. He was coming after her. They'd row, and it wouldn't be pretty. He was drunk, and probably high on something or other. Things could get nasty. She needed to move fast. Megan quickened her pace. It was difficult with all the mud. It stuck to the soles of her boots, squelching underfoot.

"Meggy!" Leon screamed into the night. "You won't get away from me so easily!"

Megan started to run. Within a few metres the ground underfoot was even worse — rutted and full of stones. She tripped, got up and took off again. She heard Leon swear. The moon dipped behind a cloud and the darkness closed in around her. She panicked. With the music echoing in her ears, Megan couldn't tell which direction Leon's voice had come from. Suddenly her foot caught in the root of a tree, and she fell headlong into a deep ditch.

Megan was momentarily stunned. The ditch was full of water — muddy, smelly stuff that made her want to retch. She floundered around trying to get to her feet. Wet through, covered in mud, squealing and spitting out the foul liquid, she finally managed to stand up. Her clothing and hair were soaked and black with mud. And there was Leon, standing on the higher ground, laughing at her.

"Not that easy to get away, is it, babe?" he taunted.

But Megan was in no mood. She stamped a foot hard on the ground, sending fetid water everywhere. "I hate you," she spat. "I hate this place. I can't do this, Leon—"

Suddenly she fell quiet. Something was floating in the water only inches away from her. She must have dislodged whatever it was from the bottom. Megan strained to see in the dark. It was weird. At first it looked like a bin bag full of festival rubbish. Moving closer, she thought it might be a piece of old wood. In the weak moonlight, its surface looked like bark.

"What on earth is it?" She looked up at Leon, who had taken several steps backwards.

"Don't go near, babe. Look. There." He pointed.

Megan peered closer and recoiled, horrified. The dim light reflected off whitish bones. The remains of an arm and a hand were visible. Tendrils of dark hair floated like weed from what had once been a human head.

Leon grabbed hold of Megan's rucksack and hauled her out. "It's a body. Been there a while too."

# Chapter 1

Day 1

"Neat place. She's got some ace stuff here," said Craig Riley. He walked around the room, running his hand over the furnishings.

The house was pristine, all clean lines done in cream and gold. In the sitting room, two top-of-the-range leather sofas and a glass coffee table with matching shelf unit. There was very little in the way of ornaments, and no photographs. This house belonged to a woman who didn't like clutter. But there were a couple of statement pieces. One was a large, chunky orange vase placed on the top shelf.

Craig Riley picked up the lump of glass and grinned. "Seen these on that antiques programme my granny watches on the telly." He tossed it casually from one hand to the other until the inevitable happened. There was a resounding crash and the vase shattered on the wooden floor, sending splinters of orange glass all over. "Oops! Silly me, slipped through my fingers."

"Shut it, Craig!" Vinny Holt snapped back. "You'll have the neighbours round."

"All at work, bro. Made sure, did my research. All this road is out during the day. Wage slaves, the bloody lot of them. We can take as long as we need."

"Where is it then, d'you reckon?" Vinny asked.

"Could be anywhere. We'll start down here, and work our way up."

"It don't look like a dealer's gaff to me."

"The tip-off was sound," Craig assured him. "You search in there." He nodded at the kitchen.

This was a woman who liked simplicity. There wasn't much furniture. In the sitting room, Craig began to look through the few drawers there were. In a carved wooden box he found a stash of jewellery and a bundle of notes. "Jackpot! Must be about a grand," he called out to Vinny.

"There's bugger all in here," Vinny called back from the kitchen. "Not even much food. Are you sure this is where she spends her time?"

"Look, I've told you. The stuff is here. But we have to find it fast. We won't get another chance. The bitch is sure to shift it soon."

The two lads both had slight, wiry frames and were dressed similarly, in trackie bottoms and a hoodie. They paid little respect to the furniture or the pride the owner obviously took in the place. The perfect house made them look even more scruffy and shifty as they slouched around.

"I'll do upstairs," Vinny decided.

Vinny Holt ran up the carpeted staircase. There were three bedrooms. He went into the largest. There was a huge bed, fitted wardrobes and drawers, all done out in the same cream and gold as downstairs. After about five minutes, he shouted down to his mate. "Nowt much up 'ere. Drawers full of clothes, can't find any more jewellery."

Vinny went to one of the wardrobes and pulled open the doors. "Found a safe," he yelled down to Craig. He got down on his knees and tried to open it.

Craig came into the room and knelt down beside him. "You won't get into that without the combination. You're wasting time. We need to crack on. Have a look in the other rooms."

"Smart place, this. Wouldn't mind one like this myself one day. What does she do, this bird?" Vinny asked.

"She works for a transport firm in town. She has an office in some posh block near the Quays. Stuck-up cow she is an' all."

"There's nowt in the bedrooms. There's no attic either."

Craig shook his head. "Where would you stash it?"

"Garage, cellar, somewhere folk don't usually go."

Craig tossed Vinny a small cloth bag containing the jewellery he'd found. "What d'you reckon to that little lot?"

"Some nice pieces. We should get a bob or two for these." A small ring caught his eye, a band of gold with a diamond inlaid at its centre. Vinny picked it out and slid it onto his little finger.

"C'mon, let's see where else we can find."

Vinny handed Craig the bag. "Back way, like we came in."

The two lads retraced their steps. They crossed the kitchen floor and found the utility room by the back door.

"Wonder if she's got booze in that fridge?" Craig nudged his mate. "She has expensive taste, might even be some of the bubbly stuff." The fridge was a huge thing, standing floor to ceiling in a corner.

"Leave it, Craig. We should check out the garage and then get out of here."

But Craig wanted a beer. He pulled the door open. There was no food or drink inside. On every shelf were three or four polythene packets, each one about thirty centimetres square. "Bingo! We've found it. This is what we came for."

Vinny already had a packet in his hands and was pulling at one corner. Very gingerly, he tasted a tiny bit of the brown powder inside. "Heroin. The bitch has a bloody fortune in heroin stashed in here."

"How d'you know?" Craig asked.

"Because I've dealt the stuff and know the taste."

Craig grinned. "Told you the info was sound. He said she was dealing."

"Dealing! Look at the stuff. This is more like trafficking. We don't hang about, mate. We take the gear and get out of here before we're caught," Vinny urged.

Craig pointed to a carrier bag hanging up behind the back door. "Pass us that. And stop stressing, there's plenty of time."

Vinny didn't move. "We're taking one mega risk. What if her place is being watched? This little lot could get us into a heap of trouble."

"Only if we're caught. Concentrate on the payoff, mate. We are going to be minted once this little lot is passed on." Craig grinned.

"Not minted enough for the risk we're taking. We deserve more than the measly share we'll get. We should keep some back, sell it ourselves," Vinny suggested. "It would make us a packet round the estate."

"No, all it'd do is bring us trouble." Craig's voice was firm. "Put the stuff in the bag!"

"What if we're caught with this little lot?" Vinny asked. "What if the law is watching this gaff?"

"No one is watching," Craig assured him. "Don't lose it now, Vinny lad. All we have to do is get back and continue with the plan. Piece of cake."

"The people this bitch messes with must be real hard nuts. We don't want them on our backs. For all we know, one of them is keeping an eye on the investment."

"I've had an idea that'll get us some insurance." Craig slapped Vinny's cheek lightly. "We get this bagged up, then we scarper, but we leave a few packets behind."

"What d'you mean? Why would that work?"

"You take a photo of the gear left in the fridge, then text it to someone along with this address. There's your insurance," said Craig.

"Text it to who?" Vinny asked.

"The police, anonymously."

Vinny stared at him.

"They come round 'ere, find the stuff, and that's us in the clear. Once the coppers are involved, everyone else will back away. The bitch that lives here will be arrested. The stuff will be too hot to handle, even for the hard nuts she's mixed up with." Craig folded his arms.

"Will that work?" Vinny asked.

"Look, soft lad, it'll work a treat. We'll be free and clear. No one will ever know that we had owt to do with it."

"Okay, but let's get gone. Best thing we can do is get this back and forget we were ever here." Vinny looked at the few packets Craig hadn't touched. "Shame though."

Craig shrugged. "Insurance, mate. We need it. And we don't tell a soul. Not even our Callum."

"Thought you might have brought him along."

"Brother or not, he can't be trusted," Craig said. "There's too much at stake. Besides, Callum has got himself roped into something at the centre today."

The lads legged it down the road to their car.

"Don't worry, I won't say owt," Vinny assured Craig. "But what about the money and other stuff we took? Won't your Callum wonder where you got the dosh from?"

"If he asks, I'll say I had a win on the dogs."

Vinny still looked worried. "What if that stuck-up bitch goes to the police after all?"

"That was heroin in the fridge, mate, not a bloody four pack! She wouldn't dare." Craig nudged him.

"I know what you said about insurance. But I've got a bad feeling about this. We've taken a fortune in heroin. Someone is bound to come looking. Think about it, Craig. This bird has got to be mixed up in some pretty heavy stuff if she's got this much stashed away. We could have anyone on our backs."

"You send the cops that picture with the address. They'll know what to do, then we're free and clear. You worry too much, that's your trouble."

"I took a pic of the house too," Vinny admitted.

"What for?"

"I've texted it to Marshy in case something goes wrong. Like you said, insurance."

Craig shook his head. "Waste of time. Marshy is an idiot."

# Chapter 2

Ava Whitton turned her dark eyes to the boardroom clock. Why did these meetings have to drag on so? Martin had been speaking almost non-stop for half an hour now. Unless someone interrupted him, he would rabbit on for the duration. She should leave. Ava had felt her phone vibrate in her jacket pocket ten minutes ago. Someone wanted her badly enough to ring during office hours. Not allowed.

"Martin?" Ava finally ventured.

Martin Greyson was the managing director and owner of the transport firm, Greyson Logistics. His word was law. He wanted to say something, you let him. Ava had just had the temerity to stop him mid-flow. All eyes turned her way.

"I have to go. Sorry, emergency at home." Ava rose to her feet, without waiting for him to agree. No doubt her colleagues would be wondering how she could possibly know about this emergency. She'd been sat at this table along with the rest of them for most of the afternoon, analysing Martin's strategic plan for the company. "You can contact me at home if necessary."

The sooner she left this job and these people, the better. But for now, it suited her purpose to play the part of the businesswoman who knew her stuff. Ava Whitton was tall and slim. She wore simple clothes to work, usually black. Her suits were always from top designers. She had a reputation for being aloof and unsympathetic. Balls-up at work and you would get nothing from her but scathing criticism. Ava was not the type of woman you confided in during lunch in the staff restaurant.

There was no ring on her finger, and she never mentioned any relationship. Ava didn't confide or speak about her personal life to anyone at work. Her women colleagues didn't like her. The men found her intriguing, despite her faults — or maybe because of them. She was very attractive. If she smiled more, she would be stunning. She had high cheekbones. Her pale blonde hair was pinned in a neat pleat at the back of her head, accentuating the shape of her face. Ava wore little make-up, a subtle perfume, high heels, and seemed always to have her nose in the air. These were the ingredients that made up her work persona.

Out in the corridor, Ava checked her mobile. It had not been a call. The vibration had been set off by an app that warned her when there was a problem at home. She had a couple of concealed cameras in her property that recorded footage that she could download onto her phone or laptop. Any time the cameras were activated by motion, she received a notification.

There had been a break-in. Ava watched wide-eyed as the two lads walked through her house and rifled through her things. They found her box containing the cash and jewellery. They went to the bedroom, then the wardrobe. They knew exactly what they were doing. She watched them try to open the safe. It made her angry, and she wanted to lash out because she was helpless. Given the circumstances, she could not even call the police. Her personal property and cash was one thing, but as she watched them open the fridge in the utility room, Ava realised she had a real problem.

* * *

PC Hough handed DS Jed Quickenden a printout "Got a strange one. Came in this morning. Could be the work of some joker, but on the other hand . . ."

DS Quickenden, universally known as 'Speedy' to his friends and colleagues, had transferred from the station in the town of Oldston to the serious crime squad on the outskirts of Manchester along with DCI Stephen Greco. He was good at his job, occasionally very good, which was why Greco had wanted him on his team. But the DS was also known to cut corners. This shortcoming had on occasion put him in danger. However, lately, he'd knuckled down and was expected to try for promotion soon.

Speedy took the printout and looked it over. "Drugs? Pretty good mock-up, if that's what it is. Where did this come from?"

"Someone texted it in this morning, along with an address. I've written that on the top."

"I'll tell the boss. We'll go and have a look," Speedy said.

Speedy took the stairs two at a time and entered the incident room on the first floor. Greco wasn't in his office — he'd gone to Manchester Central for a meeting. As for DC Grace Harper, the other member of the team, he'd no idea where she was. Grace had been frequently absent of late. She hadn't said why, and no one else had made much of it, which in this place was odd. He made for DI Leah Wells' desk and placed the paper in front of her. "What d'you think? Front desk just gave it to me. Bloody good if it's someone's idea of a joke."

Leah Wells cast a critical eye over the image. "You're thinking drugs?"

"It certainly looks like it," Speedy replied.

"There could be anything in those packets. But then again . . . ? How did we get this?"

"Arrived in the early hours of this morning. Image, address, we've even got the mobile phone number it came from. Downstairs have done the research, and got the address of the phone's owner. It's on contract to a bloke called Vinny Holt. Amateur, got to be." Speedy laughed. "No professional would make such a simple mistake."

"So, what's he been up to, this Mr Holt? And how come he was able to take this photo?"

"Want me to go and find him, ma'am? See what his game is?"

Leah Wells looked at the picture again. "Yes. Take DC Hough with you. Find Vinny Holt and have a word. Make sure he tells you where he took this. A visit to the address where they took the photo may or may not be necessary. It might be one huge joke. But if it isn't, and if there is any reluctance to let you in, ring me straight away."

"It's probably nothing. Some joker wanting to see us at it, chasing our tails."

"If it is, then we'll have him for wasting police time," Leah said. "We've got quite enough to do without that sort of thing."

She was his only company. Speedy knew he'd find Joel Hough in the canteen, having breakfast. "Grace not in yet?" he ventured.

Leah checked her watch. "No, but she won't be long."

The fact that Grace hadn't been taken to task about her recent absences made Speedy suspicious. He reckoned she was after another post somewhere else. He didn't blame her. Since she and Greco had got back from Brighton a few months ago, their relationship had been strained. Not getting on with the boss was a biggy for Grace. Not that Greco appeared to care. The bloke seemed pleased enough to be left alone. But the atmosphere in the main office had been strained lately. Where Greco was concerned, it was bad enough when everything was going smoothly. But recently, they really had to watch their step.

When Joel returned to the office, Speedy handed him the printout. "Come on, Joel, get your coat. Might be nothing, then again, we might have the deal of the century on our hands."

"Does Greco know?"

"Shouldn't think so. Better things to do, hasn't he?"

"Have you checked Vinny Holt on the system?"

"Not yet."

Joel sat at his computer to do the search. "Petty theft. Robbery, nothing too valuable and no violence. Mixes with Craig Riley. Couple of small-time villains, the both of them."

"Out of their comfort zone now then, aren't they?"

# Chapter 3

"Sorry, heavy traffic on the bypass," Stephen Greco said. He sat down next to Grace in the waiting room.

He glanced at Grace. She seemed to have accepted his apology. But the truth was, he'd deliberately taken his time. This was the day he'd been dreading. After today, what had happened between him and Grace would have a reality he wasn't ready for. Grace's pregnancy had thrown him almost as badly as Suzy's death. Greco didn't cope well with major changes. He needed routine. In order to function properly, he had to lead a strictly organised life where everything and everybody had a place. Grace's place was as a DC on his team. Not as the mother of his child.

It was ante-natal day and the small waiting room was crowded. Women in all stages of pregnancy sat and chatted. Some had their partners with them, others were alone.

"They're running late, so I'll let you off. You have been to one of these before?" Grace passed him a leaflet.

"Yes." He took the leaflet from her and slipped it into a small leather folder. "I went to all the scans when Suzy was pregnant with Matilda." What he didn't say was how very different that experience had been. He and his then wife, Suzy, had been thrilled to discover they were having a baby. Matilda had been welcomed into a home and family that loved her and wanted only to make her happy. Greco had no idea what he felt about this unborn infant. He wasn't even sure how he felt about Grace.

"Don't expect to see much. It's only the three-month one. Next time we might get to find out what sex it is." Grace looked at him. "If you want to know, that is?"

She'd picked up on his unease. He couldn't help it. Her being pregnant was a nightmare he could do without. And he was no good at feigning happiness.

"I don't mind, but it's fine with me if you do." Greco knew that he didn't sound enthusiastic. Knowing whether Grace was carrying a girl or a boy wasn't important to him. Just having to attend clinic was an inconvenience he didn't need. She was twelve weeks already, and still only the two of them knew. That situation couldn't continue for much longer.

"You could try a bit harder, Stephen. We agreed that this would be a joint effort — remember? If you're having second thoughts, let's hear them. Only it's getting a bit late to change our minds."

"No, I'm fine with it." Another lie, but he could hardly tell her the truth. He knew that Grace was looking forward to the new arrival. When they were alone together, she talked of little else. As for him, his life was full enough as it was. Greco had a job that took up most of his time, and then some. He was a single dad to a daughter who needed every spare minute he had. Throw into the mix an infant, and he had a recipe for domestic disaster. His Aunt Pat would help. No doubt she'd be delighted when they told her. But Pat was in her late fifties. She got exhausted enough running after Matilda all day long. Plus there were the implications for his work. A member of his team was pregnant with his child. Once Superintendent McCabe found out, it might mean trouble for his job. It wouldn't be so bad if he and Grace were a couple, and people thought of them as such. But they weren't, not really. The last thing Greco wanted right now was flak from his colleagues.

"You're doing my head in, d'you know that?" she said.

Greco coughed. People around them were looking. Grace was not afraid to show her irritation with him.

"You just sit there and say nowt." She punched his arm to get his attention. "Sorry if this baby is going to bugger up your orderly little world, Stephen, but that's the way it is. We talked about this. You promised it would be fine. You said you'd participate, contribute time and energy to both the pregnancy and raising our child. But you didn't mean a bloody word of it, did you? Me, the babe, we're nothing but a huge fly in the ointment. Well, you'd better come to terms with how things are pretty damn quick. Within months, this child will be born. It will have needs, and both of us will have to shape up. A combined effort, Stephen, that's what you promised."

A woman sitting opposite them was smirking. She'd heard the lot. Greco had rarely felt so embarrassed. "It's not you or the baby," he lied, "I've just been to a heavy meeting at central."

"Well, you're not at central now." Grace took hold of his arm. "You're here with me. We are going to glimpse our baby for the first time. Doesn't that mean anything? Aren't you just a little bit excited, Stephen?"

"Of course, I am." Another lie. And she spotted it. Grace turned away from him in disgust. Just at that moment, the nurse called her name.

"This is us," she said nervously. "Please try to smile."

\* \* \*

Speedy and Joel pulled up on the concrete expanse in front of the four tower blocks that made up the Lansdowne Estate.

"Vinny Holt's last address was Argo House over there. Mind you, that was over twelve months ago," Joel said.

"What floor?" Speedy asked. "Only I know for a fact that the lift's out more often than not."

"Ground floor. His mother's in a wheelchair," Joel told him.

The two detectives made their way across the rutted concrete ground. A group of kids eyed them with suspicion. Speedy turned up his overcoat collar against the biting wind. This was a desolate place even in the summer. On a bleak day in early January, it was hell. He stuffed his hands into his coat pocket. His fingers were so cold they'd gone numb.

They were surrounded by tall, featureless blocks. For as far as you could see there was nothing but concrete underfoot. There was not a tree or a patch of grass anywhere. But there was plenty of litter blowing about. No bins — too handy for drug drops, or for setting off fireworks in.

"Keep a beady on the car," said Speedy. "That lot look as if they've hit the jackpot." He nodded at a group of kids standing by the entrance. "They could have it stripped and the parts sold in a heartbeat."

DC Joel Hough stood by the entrance to the block, watching the car across the square, while a few metres away, Speedy banged on the door of the Holt address. A man answered. He looked about forty, rough, and had a fag hanging out of his mouth.

"That was bloody quick. I've only just rung the station. Have you found our kid yet? She's going off her head with worry."

"Found who?" Speedy asked.

The man looked the detective up and down. "The lad. Our Vinny. He went out last night and we haven't seen 'im since. He's not the perfect lad, but he always comes home. I rang his mate Craig. Can't find him either. Wouldn't normally bother. Chances are they've dossed down somewhere. But she's a worrier. Best keep her happy, eh?"

"Who are you?" Speedy asked.

"Dave Holt, Vinny's big brother. I'm having to stay with her." He nodded back through the door. "In a right state, Mum is."

The kids who had been lurking at the entrance had gone so Joel joined them. "When exactly did you last see Vinny?" he asked.

"Last night, about five. He came here, Craig in tow, and said they were going to get tea from the chippy. When he didn't come back I thought they must have gone for a game of pool."

"Is that usual for him?"

"No, he always comes home. Too fond of his own bed."

"Did you have an argument with him? Was he okay when he left?"

"We didn't row, and he was fine. Dead happy in fact. He bunged mum fifty quid too. Said he'd had a win on the dogs."

"Where does he hang out?"

"The Grapes, and he plays pool down the community centre."

Speedy had a bad feeling. The photo of the house. The drugs. The lads could have stumbled into something they couldn't handle. "Do you have a recent photo of him?" Speedy asked. "We'll get it circulated."

"Wait 'ere, I'll get one. Don't want her upsetting all over again." He disappeared inside.

"So where are they?" Joel asked.

"We'll have a word with Craig's family next," Speedy said. "You never know, Vinny might be there. Had a skinful and dossed down for the night."

A woman was walking towards them. "Is he here?" she shouted. "Only our Craig hasn't come home. Silly bugger's got a job interview this afternoon too."

19

"No, he isn't." Speedy assumed she meant Craig Riley. "And neither is Vinny. The two of them seem to have done one. Who are you?"

"Craig's mother. I'll kill him if he misses the chance of work. Cock this up and he'll not get back in the house. Bloody hard going, he is. I've got two of 'em, couldn't be more different. Our Callum's a right good lad, but Craig . . . more trouble than he's worth at times. Bad tempered. Got a short fuse."

"When did you see him last?"

"Late on yesterday afternoon. Him and Vinny were coming here, then going off somewhere together."

Dave Holt reappeared with a photo. "This is the pair of them. Taken about a month ago on Mum's birthday."

"Okay, we'll get onto it straight away. But if either of them turns up, ring us at once." Speedy handed cards to Dave Holt and Craig's mother.

# Chapter 4

Greco looked at the image from different angles. The grey outline was barely visible. A baby? It didn't look like one yet.

Grace took it from him. "I'll get you a copy of your own. Something else for your little folder." She grinned. "I wonder who it will look like? Boy or girl, it is bound to have blond hair. If it's a boy, I hope he has your looks."

Greco ignored this. "Are you coming to work?"

"Yes, but I'm in my own car so we needn't arrive together." She kissed his cheek. "Try and be happy about the little one, Stephen. It will make life much easier."

Greco watched her walk off down the corridor. Grace had no idea what a hard ask that was. She was thrilled about the baby. He'd seen her face when the image first came up on the screen. Then, when they'd heard the baby's heart beating, she had tears in her eyes. Why didn't he feel like that? Because it was all wrong, that was why.

Perhaps if their relationship had been less one-sided? Grace had made no secret of the fact that she liked him and had made all the running. After Brighton, when she'd told him about the baby, he'd taken her out a couple of times. Grace had loved that, but he hadn't been so keen. He'd done it because he felt he should, and not from any real desire. Grace was a friend, a good detective and someone he trusted. But did he want her for his wife? Being the man he was, Greco knew he'd have to consider it. She was having his child. He could not watch her struggle through it alone. Plus, marrying Grace would solve the problem of the infant, and consolidate the two families. His daughter, Matilda, and Holly, Grace's daughter, would love it. They were the same age, went to the same school and were best friends.

His mobile rang. It was Speedy.

"We've got two missing teenage lads, guv. Both eighteen, both live on the Lansdowne. That photo we got this morning could be significant. I forwarded it to your mobile earlier. The one which showed what looked like a stash of drugs in a fridge. It came with an address. The lad who sent it to us and his mate haven't been seen since yesterday teatime. Joel and I are about to go to the house. It's a posh job in Cheshire, Handforth way. D'you want to meet us there?"

Greco thought for a moment. He'd glanced at the image and the text, but then thought no more of it, wanting to get the scan sorted before he turned his mind to anything else. Speedy and Joel were more than capable of speaking to whoever lived at that address themselves. On the other hand, it did mean he could avoid the station and Grace for a little longer. "I'm in Oldston, so give me half an hour or so to get there. But don't start without me."

Greco could only guess what it all meant. If the motive for being in the house was robbery, then the lads could have taken off somewhere on the proceeds. Then again, with drugs involved, perhaps they'd bitten off more than they could chew.

Greco left Oldston and made for the M60. Once Greater Manchester was left behind, the view became more pleasant, with fields instead of row upon row of old terraced houses, industrial estates and shops. Away from the dual carriageway there were villages and open views. Given its relative proximity to his job in town, Greco began to wonder why he wasn't living out here. If he decided to make a go of it with Grace, a place like one of these would make a perfect home for the children.

It was a large detached property on a well-spaced-out development of a dozen similar houses. The owner obviously had money and didn't mind spending it.

Speedy and Joel Hough were waiting in their car outside the house.

"There is someone in, guv," Speedy said. "I've seen movement through the window."

"Okay, let's get this done with." Greco strode up the path with the other two following behind. He pressed the bell and waited. Speedy fumbled in his overcoat pocket for the photo.

The woman who answered the door was tall and blonde. Immaculate in a dark suit with a knee-length skirt. Her expression was stony.

"What do you want?"

Greco was staring. He couldn't help it. He was taken completely by surprise. He wasn't sure what he'd been expecting, but it wasn't someone like this. She was perfect, quite flawless. His height in her high heels, and slim, she was about as far from a drug dealer as he could imagine.

She met his stare with cool brown eyes. Eyes that made him nervous. He coughed. "DCI Greco. This is DS Quickenden and DC Hough. We're from the serious crime squad in Manchester."

For several seconds she stood in silence. She didn't even blink. Finally, she said, "I'm Ava Whitton."

"Can we come in?" Greco asked. "I'd like to ask you a couple of questions."

"What — all of you? You want to trample through my home after being out in that filthy weather?"

It was late January and sleeting. Greco looked down at his feet. "We can take off our shoes if it'll make you feel better."

He could hear Speedy muttering behind him. But Greco wasn't bothered. Given his own hang-ups, he understood the woman's concerns. He looked along the elegant hallway to the plush, cream carpet. With their dirty, wet, feet the three of them would ruin it in seconds.

"Leave your shoes there." She pointed to the mat by the door. "I do not have long. I need to get back to work."

Without a word, Greco followed her along the hall. Her clothes were expensive, and there wasn't a hair out of place on her beautiful head. Right then, he would have happily done anything she asked. This was a new one for him. The only other woman who'd affected him this way had been Suzy. When they first met, he'd been so nervous he'd stammered.

"What is it you do?" Greco asked her.

"I am the transport manager for a logistics firm in town — Greysons."

They entered the sitting room, decorated tastefully in cream and gold. The place was as perfect as she was. There wasn't a speck of dust, and nothing was out of place. He could live here with no effort at all. Every cushion was plumped, each surface gleaming and pristine. This was a woman he could understand, and who would understand him too.

"Lovely home, you have."

"I know," she said matter-of-factly, and turned and regarded the three men. "So, what can I do for you?"

Speedy thrust the picture at her. "Do you know anything about this?"

Greco watched her eyes. Not a flicker.

"No. What am I supposed to see? What do those packets contain?"

"Drugs of some sort, possibly," Speedy said. "The message that accompanied it said the photo had been taken in this house."

"Here? In my home? Are you mad?" Ava Whitton said.

"Have you had a break-in during the past day or so?" Speedy asked.

"No. I would have called the police if I had"

"We are acting on information given to us. We know who took that picture, and we suspect they were here to rob you," Greco said.

"You are mistaken. There is nothing missing. Neither is there any sign of a robbery. If you look at that image closely you'll spot that it shows nothing of the surroundings. It could have been taken anywhere."

Greco said nothing, mesmerised by the sound of her voice. He thought her accent sounded vaguely foreign.

Ava Whitton's hands were on her hips. "This is ridiculous. Who do you think I am?" She sighed. "Come with me."

They followed her without demur from the sitting room, through a spotless ultra-modern kitchen and into a room off at the side.

"This is the utility room where I keep my fridge and freezer. Look for yourself."

Greco pulled open the door.

"You may examine it all you want, but there is nothing in it but food. That's all."

She was right. A bog-standard fridge with the usual contents. "We're sorry to have troubled you. We have to investigate. I hope you understand," Greco said.

"You've had a wasted journey. For whatever reason, someone is obviously having a joke at your expense."

"Do you have a security camera, Ms Whitton?"

"No," she replied sharply.

They followed her back the way they had come. Passing through the sitting room, Joel Hough stopped to look out of the window. He put his hands on a glass table-top to steady himself. "Lovely view you have here. You can see the hills in the distance."

"Get your hands off that! The glass marks easily." Ava Whitton took a handkerchief from her pocket and rubbed the surface vigorously.

"She's a bloody neat freak like him," Speedy whispered in Joel's ear.

# Chapter 5

Day 2

Between Openshaw Road — where the serious crime squad was based — and the M60, there was a network of streets of old terraced houses. Between each row were small passageways, called ginnels. These narrow passageways were all interconnected. It was in one of these that the bodies were found dumped next to a skip. Both bodies were a ravaged, beaten mess.

A resident had called it in. He had been dumping rubbish in a skip when he spotted them. The sight was ghastly. He described the way they looked 'as if they'd been got at by a bunch of wild animals.' A uniformed PC swiftly arrived. He put up a tent, taped off the immediate area, and waited in a squad car for the circus to begin.

It didn't take long. A team from the Duggan, headed by Dr Bob Bowers, the pathologist, and Roxy Atkins, the forensic scientist, was next to turn up. Within minutes of their arrival, Greco and Speedy were at the scene.

"Unrecognisable, guv." The colour had drained from Speedy's face. "That poor bugger is missing an eye, and the rest of his face has been mutilated. Hit with something hard it looks like. Broke all the bones — jaw and cheek. The other one has been slashed open from ear to ear."

Greco said nothing.

"The victims Craig Riley and Vinny Holt," Roxy told them. "Well, they are at present. We'll need to confirm that. Both are naked, and given the extent of the mutilation it is difficult to tell. But the killer was thoughtful enough to write their names across their chests in felt tip."

Greco could only marvel at her even, matter-of-fact tone. Though he might not be showing it, he was a long way from feeling matter of fact right now.

"What has happened to their hands?" he said.

Bob Bowers looked up at him. "Their fingers are missing, Stephen. At first glance it looks like they've been tortured." That was stating the obvious. "However, there is very little blood around the wounds."

"This is where they were dumped. The kill site will be where the blood is," Greco said.

"And they have been set alight," Speedy added.

"Nonetheless, I'll reserve judgement until the PM. If it was torture, then it was protracted and vicious. If it wasn't — why bother mutilating corpses?"

"What's that?" Speedy pointed to a plastic bag containing what looked like something unnameable from the butchers.

"Don't touch — and I wouldn't look too closely either," said Roxy. "It's not been photographed yet." She took a deep breath. "I suspect it contains body parts of the victims."

Speedy's face contorted in horror.

* * *

Back at the Serious Crime Unit on Gorton Road, Greco assembled the team for a briefing.

"Prior to the discovery of the two bodies this morning, we had nothing but the photo and the address they sent in the text. Given what was done to them, it looks highly likely that Craig Riley and Vinny Holt witnessed or took something that angered someone enough to merit their possible torture and murder. If those packets in the fridge did contain drugs, that may be our motive."

"So, we are going with the premise that it is them?" Joel Hough asked.

"We'll get confirmation from the Duggan soon enough. Both of the lads have been in trouble previously, so it's likely their DNA and fingerprints are on record."

Joel Hough nodded.

"Of course," Greco said, "we have no proof that the packets contained anything of the kind. We only have the text to go on. That, and the image we were sent have been investigated and the owner questioned. But in view of what has happened to the lads, we have to give the picture credence. We will look a lot closer at both the house and Ava Whitton." Greco wrote her name on the board. "We paid the woman a cursory visit earlier and got nowhere. She was happy enough to show us the fridge and didn't appear to have anything to hide. However, it would be a simple matter to clean the fridge and fill it with food. Presuming the drugs were stolen, she is hardly going to report the theft. What we do now is send in forensics. If there have been drugs in that fridge or anywhere near, they will tell us. If Ms Whitton won't play ball, we get a warrant."

Superintendent McCabe entered the room. "That could prove tricky," he said. "All you have is that photo. There is nothing on it to prove where it was taken. You can't even make out what sort of fridge it is, other than it's one of those tall ones. Ms Whitton could argue that it was the work of some prankster and refuse to allow the search. Our evidence is very thin."

"Stealing the drugs is the only motive we've got, sir. Holt and Riley were small-time," Greco said. "They've done nothing that we are aware of to attract the violence that was done to them. Whoever did that wanted something from them badly enough to torture and kill. The only explanation that makes sense, given what we've got, is that they took drugs from the house in Handforth. And whoever they took them from wanted them back."

"What's she like?" Grace whispered to Speedy.

"A peach," Speedy whispered back. "Despite her suspected involvement, he liked her, I could tell. You'll see what I mean when you meet her. She's like him, a stickler for everything in its place and dead clean."

Greco was getting annoyed. Speedy was gossiping to Grace, and from the look on her face, he knew what it was about. "Whatever your opinion, Sergeant Quickenden, Ms Whitton is a person of interest, nothing else. Gossiping won't help matters." Greco saw Grace's frown and knew Speedy had probably told her about his reaction when he first saw the woman. No doubt with embellishments. The last thing he needed was jealousy in the incident room.

Grace changed the subject. "The victims' families? Have they been told?"

"My next job is to visit them." He nodded at her. "You can come with me. Speedy, find out all you can about Ava Whitton. I want a full rundown of her life over the last few years. What she does, who she knows, financial status, you know the stuff. Anything suspicious, anything at all, let me know. It is a priority for us to link that woman and that house to the lads. Leah, you and Joel get as much background as you can on Riley and Holt. Find out what they were up to. We know that they weren't whiter than white. Given their history of low-level crime, they must have learned about the stash of drugs from someone. That 'someone' could have done the organising. We need to know who they had been knocking about with recently. Once they had the drugs, the pair either withheld them or a rival dealer got at them. Whoever took and killed those young men wanted something from them.

30

Hence the torture. We need to know for sure what that was."

Superintendent Gordon McCabe stood looking at the incident board, waiting for Greco to finish briefing the team. He shook his head. "Bad business. Not much to work with either. If you want my opinion, those lads stumbled into something big."

Everything the team had so far was written neatly on the board. All the images, including those of the lads, were pinned down the right-hand side. McCabe ran his eyes over them, and tapped the picture of Ava Whitton. "This one has to know more than she's saying. House like that, I bet she's got security too, a camera, maybe." He turned to Greco. "If she has, think she'll part with it?"

"I asked, and she said not. Ms Whitton wasn't having any of it when we visited yesterday. In her opinion we were barking up the wrong tree entirely. However, those neighbours of hers probably have cameras. I'll get on it, see what we come up with."

"You think those young men took the drugs?"

"Yes, I do, and not only drugs. Vinny Holt's older brother said that Vinny had cash in his pocket when he saw him last. It's likely that Ava Whitton had money or other valuables around the house. If the drugs were there, they may have kept some packets back for themselves. We just don't know yet."

McCabe peered at the image Vinny Holt had texted. "You could be right. There must be half a dozen packets in there, but there is room for a helluva lot more. Dealing in a big way like that takes a lot of organisation."

"I know. That would mean that there was money around. Perhaps even a safe. We need to take a closer look at that house."

McCabe looked at the images of Vinny and Craig at the dump site. "Whoever did that is an animal. He needs catching, and quick. Have a word with the drug squad, see if they know anything."

* * *

"The two of them hung out at the Grapes, and the community centre on the Lansdowne. Since that's nearest, we'll go there first," Leah said.

Joel was driving. He pulled out onto Openshaw Road, took a left and within a few hundred yards the tower blocks loomed in front of them. "The community centre is that single-storey building to the far right," he said. "A bloke called Graham Clovelly runs it. All sorts of activities go on there. He tries to do as much as he can for the young people on this estate."

"Sounds like a good bloke. Know him?"

"He asked me to have a chat with the teenagers a while ago. About drugs and booze, you know the stuff. The centre does a good job, fills a gap. Seems to be working. Things have been quiet around here for a while now."

Leah wondered how DC Joel Hough had gone down with the locals. They were a rough lot, and he was a world away from them. Joel was young, studious, keen on his job. His heavy-rimmed glasses gave him a geeky look. She could imagine the lads who frequented the place making taking the piss.

"I've just had a text from Grace. She and Greco are about to tell the families," Leah told Joel. "So we can get moving. According to DCI Greco, Craig and Vinny played pool here. But their friends are unlikely to know what's happened yet, so we'll tread gently."

The building was divided into two rooms with a small café area between. There was an exercise class going on in one of them, and in the other a man was sorting the pool tables and stashing the cues.

Joel introduced him to Leah. "This is Graham."

She smiled at him. "I'm DI Wells. Can we go somewhere quiet? We'd like to ask you a few questions."

Graham Clovelly looked her up and down, then led the way to a table in the corner of the café. "Nothing heavy, I hope. I've a lot to do, getting things ready for the match this evening. We're taking on the Oldston senior team for a place in the league."

"Did you know Craig Riley and Vinny Holt?" Leah asked.

Graham didn't pick up on her use of the past tense. "Yes, of course I do. Regulars of mine. Good lads underneath all that front. Vinny's got himself straightened out. In fact, recently both him and Craig have joined my group of 'angels.'"

Leah looked at him. "Angels?"

"We do a lot of things at the centre, but we don't get a lot of funding," he explained. "I had the idea of recruiting the youngsters to help. And it works. They help with the classes, the youth club for the younger kids, and the discos on a Friday night. One of them had the bright idea of calling themselves 'community angels,' and it stuck. Keeps them out a trouble — win-win all round, I'd say."

Joel nodded. "I agree, Graham."

"Craig and Vinny — not got themselves into bother, have they? Only I need the pair of them for later, for the game. They're both good players."

There was no easy way to say it, so Joel simply told him. "They're both dead, Graham."

Graham turned pale. "I don't understand. What on earth happened? Did they have an accident? They weren't mucking about with that car again, were they? Craig was always trying to soup it up."

Joel shook his head. "No. They were brutally murdered. They were found this morning. Don't go spreading it around until we're sure our colleagues have told their families."

Graham turned paler still. "Murdered. I know they used to cut it a bit fine at times, but they must have crossed someone really bad for things to go that far. Do you know what happened? Have you arrested anyone?"

"No, not yet," said Leah. "But investigations are ongoing. We could do with your help. We need to know what they were into. Who they knocked around with."

Graham Clovelly looked away across the room. The exercise class had broken up, and a young man was pulling the tables back into place and setting out laptops on them. "They knew most of the younger end that come here, Marshy in particular. That's Marshy in there, one of our 'angels.' He runs the IT group. Mostly for old folk who've never had the chance to learn. He'll know what was going on with Vinny and Craig. The three of them were together a lot recently."

The young man was tall and skinny with straight dark hair down to his shoulders. He was wearing jeans and a sweater. Leah looked across at him just as a young woman joined him. They appeared to be arguing.

"That's Dee. She helps out too sometimes, does lunches for the elderly and stuff. And like Marshy, she helps with the English class. Marshy has a soft spot for her. Gets a bit possessive, which causes the odd problem because Dee has some other boy on the go. Smart type, with a flash office job."

"English class?" Leah asked.

"See that block over there?" Graham pointed. "Most of the flats are occupied by Eastern Europeans. Dee is great with them. She even knows a few phrases in some of the languages. Enough to make herself understood. There are kids in that block from Romania and Poland who've got no English at all. They are thrown straight into our school system, which is not geared up to deal with them. We had an Iraqi lad who started at the local comp. They didn't have an interpreter. Dee stepped in, found someone in the community and got the lad the help he needed. Marshy and her work well together."

"Would you ask him to come over?" Leah said.

Graham went over to speak to him.

Once Graham was out of earshot, Leah whispered, "Despite all that goody-goody stuff, they are still a weird-looking couple. Not my idea of angels, but if it's keeping them all out of trouble, who am I to criticise? She looks a right oddball. Look at that hair." She nodded at Dee.

Dee's hair was bleached almost white and spiky. She was in her mid-twenties, and her face was heavily made up. Her eyes were ringed with thick lines of mascara.

Joel laughed. "I can't imagine either of them teaching pensioners or immigrants. But Graham obviously trusts them."

Leah decided to reserve judgement for now. Marshy approached their table. "What's your full name?" she asked.

"Max Marsh," he replied, looking wary.

"Hence the nickname, 'Marshy.'"

He nodded. "What's this about? What's happened? Why are you lot on my back?"

He'd guessed they were police. "Your mates Craig and Vinny," Leah asked, "can you tell me what they've been up to recently?"

He shrugged. "Nowt much. Hang out here a lot, in the café, waiting for me. Then we might go to the Grapes, grab a beer. Nowt special."

"Did they have any enemies? Had they upset anyone recently?"

"No idea. I don't think so. Why not go and ask them?"

"Because they are both dead, Max," Joel told him. "And they didn't die of natural causes."

Marshy's eyes widened. "You're saying they were killed? Why? Who'd want them dead?"

"That's why we're here. We thought you might be able to help us."

Marshy shook his head vigorously. "I know nowt. We knew each other, but everybody knows everybody around here. Me, I try to mind my own business." He backed away. "I don't get involved in anything dodgy. I can't help, sorry. I'm needed in there. My group will be starting soon."

Leah held up a hand. "We didn't say they were involved in anything. Because the truth is, we don't know. So why did you say that?"

He shrugged again. "Got themselves murdered, stands to reason. They must have upset someone with a short fuse."

He turned on his heel and walked away.

"Rattled?" Leah asked.

Joel nodded. "Just a bit."

# Chapter 6

"This woman you met today. The one with the drugs. Speedy reckons you like her," Grace said.

Greco knew this was coming. "No, I thoughts she was *different*, that's all."

"In what way different, Stephen? As in, 'fancy her' *different?*"

"No, of course not," he protested. "She surprised me, that's all."

"What do you mean?"

"Drugs, and dealing them, it conjures up a certain type of person. She was not it. That's all it was."

They were driving towards the Lansdowne to speak to the families of the two dead lads. It was a hard enough situation without having an argument with Grace. A change of tactic was needed.

"Would you and Holly like to come for tea tonight?"

The reaction was instant. Her face lit up. Grace was really pretty when she smiled. She should smile more often. Recently she'd done something to her hair. Greco took another glance at her. That was it. She'd had it cut. It was no longer scraped back in that unflattering ponytail.

Now it framed her face in a wavy bob. She'd put on a bit of weight too. It softened her features.

"Pat is doing something special." This was a fib, but he had to cheer Grace up. "I thought we could break the news to her."

"I'd love it," she said. "But I have to tell my mum about the baby too, don't forget."

"Bring her along. We'll tell them all together — Pat, your mum, and the girls. Do some more copies of the scan picture too. They're all bound to want one."

The atmosphere changed instantly. The right thing to do? He'd no idea, but there was no going back. The baby was a fact. It was time he faced up to that.

"The Holt family are not whiter than white, you know," Grace warned him. "Vinny's brother has been inside for dealing."

"You think what happened to the lads had something to do with him?" asked Greco.

"Who knows, but he mixes with some dangerous types."

"We'll just get the hard part over with for now. Once they know what's happened, we can come back and ask questions."

* * *

Craig Riley's mother and brother lived in a two-storey maisonette on the second floor of Trojan house. Agnes Riley didn't take the news well.

"I was angry with him," she wailed. "I thought he'd done a runner because of the job."

"Do you know where he went yesterday, Mrs Riley?" Grace asked.

"He went off somewhere with Vinny. Out all day, came home and got changed then went off again. He never tells me owt. Always been the same."

Just at that moment a young man came in from another room. Grace gasped and grabbed Greco's arm.

"It's him! It's Craig! I've seen the photo. It is him. But how can that be?"

Agnes Riley gave a strained little laugh. "Hard work as he was, I wish it was our Craig, love. But it's not. This is Callum. Identical they are, well, to look at. Not in other ways though, thank God."

"You're Craig's twin?" Greco tried to work out what this might mean, if anything. "Were you close? Did you know what he was up to?"

Callum Riley shook his head. "Didn't tell me owt. Reckoned I was a grass. We used to knock about a lot, but after he got close to Vinny I gave up on them both. The Holts are a bad lot." He shrugged. "Look what's happened now."

"Where were you yesterday, Callum?" Greco asked.

"I helped out at the centre with the food bank. The bulk of the vouchers had been given out that morning, so we were at it most of the day."

"Do you know where your brother went last night?"

"Out with that no-hoper, Holt. It'll have been to the Grapes or into town. He didn't tell me. Twins, yes. In each other's pockets — no."

"What happens now?" Agnes Riley asked. "When do we arrange his funeral?"

"We'll let you know," Grace told her kindly. "Take my card. If you remember anything else, ring me."

\* \* \*

When Greco told Dave Holt what had happened to his brother, his face turned white. He started shaking, and clung on to the back of a chair to steady himself. "What do I tell her? This is bad. Mum isn't well. It'll finish her." He nodded at the door to the next room. "You can't tell her. I'll have to do that. Vinny was always her baby, her favourite — you know how it is."

"Given what has happened, we need to find out what Vinny was doing over the past couple of days, and who he might have been with. We are hoping that you can help with that."

"Whatever he was up to, he'd have had Craig Riley in tow. The two of them were into all sorts. But nothing heavy. Vinny didn't cope well when I was inside, neither did Mum. He knew better than to take risks." He thought for a moment. "But he must have been up to something. He borrowed my car. I had just put petrol in the thing too. I reckon he did about forty miles all told. Tank was half empty when he got back. Never said where he was going either."

"You told my colleague that Vinny had money when he got home. He gave his mother fifty pounds. Did he say where he got it from?" asked Grace.

"Said he'd had a win at the dogs. I had no reason to suspect he was lying."

"Does he use the betting shop down the road?"

Dave nodded.

"Can we take a look at his room?" Greco asked.

Dave led the way upstairs. Vinny's room was at the back of the flat. It contained a single bed, a chest of drawers and a small wardrobe. It was very small and the paintwork was tatty. The window looked out onto a patch of waste ground.

"Look through what you want," Dave told them. "I'll have to tell Mum. She'll wonder what you're doing here again. She will be devastated."

Once they were alone, Grace asked, "What are you thinking?"

"Someone tortured those lads. That means they wanted something from them. That something could be here."

Grace went through the drawers while Greco looked in the wardrobe.

"Nothing in these but clothes. There is a suitcase up there." She pointed to the top of the wardrobe.

Greco reached up and lifted it down. It was empty. "Nothing in the wardrobe either."

"Not here then. No money or drugs. We should check out that bookies."

Greco's phone rang. It was Speedy. He put the phone on speaker so Grace could hear.

"The tech boys have been on. We now have all the activity for the last few days on Vinny and Craig's mobiles. Vinny Holt sent the picture of the packets of drugs to us. He also sent a picture of Ava Whitton's house to someone called Marshy. One word — 'house' — and the image."

"That information, plus we now know they did a forty-mile round trip in the car, which could have taken them out to Handforth," Greco said. "Ava Whitton. Got anything?"

"She has no online presence, sir. No Facebook, no Twitter, nothing. Unusual in this day and age."

"Check if she has Wi-Fi at that house of hers. Maybe she uses another name."

"Still like her?" Grace said dryly.

\* \* \*

Once the class broke up, Marshy squared up to Dee. "The lecky bill came today and I've got nowt to pay it with."

She smirked at him, her hands in the pockets of her jeans. Jeans so tight that, along with the skin-hugging top she wore, Dee looked like a stick insect with a spiky head.

"You said you'd help. You doss down at the place often enough. You said you'd share the rent and the bills, remember?"

"You'll have to wait till the end of the week. I'll get some money then. My fella will help us out." She nudged him in the chest. "What happened to that neat little scam you had going? Not ballsed it up, surely?"

His face had fallen at the mention of her boyfriend. Now it fell further. "That had nothing to do with me. I told you. I was never part of it. It was down to that pair of losers."

"Rubbish! You are up to your neck in something. I know you. Whatever it is, it's come unstuck."

Marshy didn't want to talk about it. "Take this." He handed her a gold necklace. "Surely you can lend me something on this? It's valuable."

He watched Dee examine the piece. It was a gold chain bearing a round pendant with a ruby border. "Got to be worth a oner."

"I've not got a oner to give you. If you want that much, you'll have to sell it yourself."

"I can't do that. The police would be on my back within hours. I've got history, remember. Every pawnbroker in the area has got my mugshot hanging in their shop."

She fished in her jeans pockets and pulled out two twenties. "This will have to do. If you need more, you'll have to sell summat else. Some of that stuff you smoke. Those kids outside will pay good money for class gear."

"Can't do that. Promised Graham I'd give all that up."

"Bet you haven't. Well, more fool you if you have. In that case, get it off those mates of yours. The stupid one always has money in his pocket."

Marshy didn't know if she meant Craig or Vinny, but it didn't matter, it made him angry. "Those mates of mine are dead. Murdered!" He spat the words at her. "We've had the police here asking questions. So get off my back, Dee. I'm in no mood."

Dee's face turned pale. "So that's what the coppers wanted. Looking for answers, were they?"

"They want to know what the pair of them was up to."

"Did you tell them?"

"I don't know anything."

She looked as anxious as he felt. "You're lying," she said. "You do know something. It's written all over your face. What is it?"

"I told you. Nothing. Get off my back."

"Whatever it is, my advice is, keep quiet. If the cops get wind they won't let you off the hook so lightly. If they find out you know something about who killed that pair, they'll have you."

Marshy shook his head. "Keep your mouth shut, Dee. I don't know anything, not really."

"No worries, bro. But show an interest and they'll poke around in your past. Given your record, next thing they'll pin the lot on you. You'd be handing them an easy way out. Stick to what you're good at, Marshy."

"What about the lecky bill?"

Dee shrugged her narrow shoulders and walked off. Marshy felt cheated. The necklace was a bonus. He knew what Dee was like. She'd give it a few days, then sell it.

# Chapter 7

"You might have given me more notice, Stephen," Pat Greco complained. "Anyway, I've done roast beef, with apple pie for afters. What d'you think?"

Greco kissed her cheek. "It'll be great. Your food is always wonderful."

"What about Grace? She isn't veggie or anything, is she? Only she's a skinny one."

"Grace will eat anything," he assured her.

"You've asked her mother along too?"

Greco knew that his aunt was fishing for more information. This was all last minute, not like him at all. Greco's usual way was careful planning. Events were marked on the calendar weeks in advance, and every detail worked out well before. Impromptu gatherings were just not his thing.

"I thought it would be a nice thing to do."

"No, you didn't. Something's going on. I know you, Stephen, and this isn't like you. You don't hide things well. Ever since you and Grace took off to Brighton, you've been different."

"We didn't take off. It was work. You're right, though," he admitted, "there is something. But I can't say anything until Grace and her family get here. It wouldn't be fair."

Greco saw the smile. Pat was pleased. She was jumping to conclusions again. His aunt would like nothing better than to see him settled down with a woman. And she liked Grace.

"Will we need that bottle of champagne we didn't open on my birthday?" she asked.

He smiled. "We might."

Greco's six-year-old daughter, Matilda, rushed into the room. She was wearing a flouncy, yellow taffeta and lace dress. She did a twirl. "My Belle dress. Holly is going to wear hers. We're going to be twinnies," she announced, and ran towards Pat, who was setting the dining table.

Greco followed her. "You like Holly, don't you?"

"She's my bestest friend. We want to go on holiday together next summer. We've been doing about the seaside at school and we decided."

The front doorbell rang. Matilda let out a whoop. They were here. Greco's stomach tightened. This was it, no going back.

\* \* \*

"There was a helluva ruck going on. That one," the desk sergeant nodded at Dave Holt, "had one poor bugger pinned down and was about to lamp him with a beer bottle. If our lot hadn't been called, he could've killed the bloke."

"Was this in the Grapes?" Speedy knew that this was likely to be Holt's preferred pub.

"No, the Ashtree on Gorton Road."

"Do we know what it was about?" Speedy asked.

"No. Holt has been tight-lipped since we brought him in. I thought you should know, given you're working on his brother's murder. Also, the bloke Holt was arguing with is a well-known fence. The Ashtree is his local. Holt usually drinks in the Grapes. It struck me that he went looking for the bloke."

"What sort of stuff does he fence?"

"Specialises in antiques and jewellery," the desk sergeant replied.

Speedy nodded. "Okay. Holt should have calmed down by now. I'll have a word. See if he'll tell me what's going on."

But Dave Holt wasn't saying anything much. He sat looking at the floor. "Bloke annoyed me, simple as that. Said our Vinny deserved what he got."

"Not nice." Speedy shook his head. "You know the bloke. He fences jewellery. Did you go looking for him? Perhaps you were you trying to sell him something? Something Vinny left behind before he went missing? Or something he gave you to look after?"

Holt's head shot up. "That's not how it was. You've got it all wrong. I've got nowt to sell. Vinny didn't have anything of value."

"Are you sure? Maybe something he acquired recently, at a house in Cheshire, for example?"

"You're talking out of your backside, copper. Our Vinny had a win on the dogs, nowt else."

A uniformed officer tapped on the interview door. "The bloke he attacked, Bert Banister. He isn't pressing charges. And the landlord reckons there was no damage done."

So that was that. They couldn't keep him. This was going nowhere. "You're lucky this time, Dave. You can go."

Speedy had no idea what it all meant, but he decided to ring Greco and tell him anyway. The boss liked to know things ASAP.

\* \* \*

"Pregnant!" Emily Harper exclaimed, looking first at Grace, then at Greco. "How long?"

"About three months, Mum," Grace replied.

"And you're all right with it? After what happened before?"

Grace looked at Greco for support. "Well, yes. Stephen and I will be fine. He isn't Jack, Mum. He won't run out on us."

Emily Harper had a worried frown on her face. Greco could see that she was not convinced. She was afraid for her daughter, and given the history, that was only natural. Grace had raised Holly on her own. The child's father had run off before she was even born. Emily had had to step into the breach, and had done it wonderfully. Greco's auntie Pat, on the other hand, was delighted.

"Just what you need, Stephen! A fresh start." She beamed. "I'm so pleased for you both."

"I won't let Grace down," Greco assured Emily. "We'll be a family, all of us."

"Will you get married?" Pat asked.

Trust her to come out with that one. But the truth was, Greco wasn't sure. He was considering his reply when his mobile rang. It was Speedy.

Without answering Pat, he left the table and went into his study to take the call. Guessing it was work, Grace followed him. They left the others talking, thrashing out between them what they had just been told.

"We'll keep an eye on him," Greco told his sergeant. "Holt is a tricky one. His behaviour suggests that he knows more than he's told us."

"I had to let him go. No one wanted to take it further."

"Typical. We'll have a word tomorrow."

Meanwhile, Grace had been looking round. "I don't think I've been in here before," she said when he'd finished talking.

This was Greco's private place. His neat little haven away from the turmoil of the rest of the house. His desk was in here and his laptop, everything carefully laid out in its place.

"What are these?" Grace had noticed a series of charts on the wall.

"Family history stuff. It's my thing." He saw the little smile that hovered on her lips. "I know what you're thinking. Boring and all that." He folded his arms. "But it keeps me sane."

"I wasn't thinking anything. I think it's fascinating stuff. How far back have you got?"

"With the Greco line, not as far as I thought. It's an unusual name, so I expected it to be relatively easy. I was wrong. But I keep fishing."

Grace changed the subject. "I think tonight is going okay, don't you?"

"We'll see. Your mum might have something to say when she gets you alone."

"She'll be fine. She likes babies." Grace laughed.

They returned to the dining room. The mood was lighter. Emily Harper was laughing. She had a copy of the scan picture in her hands and was showing it to Holly.

"We are going to have a baby sister," Matilda told him. "It's growing in Grace's tummy." She paused for a moment, a puzzled look on her young face. "Won't that mean it's Holly's sister, not mine?"

"No, Tilly," Greco bent down. "You see it takes a mummy and a daddy to make babies, and I'm the baby's daddy."

"That's okay, then." She smiled.

"But it might not be a sister. We might have a brother for you both. How would you feel about that?"

Matilda pulled a face. "I suppose a brother would be okay. But he'll have to play proper with us."

"That was work," Greco explained to the adults. "My sergeant wanting to keep me in the loop." He turned to

Grace. He hadn't actually told her about the conversation yet. "Dave Holt has been brought in. He was fighting in a pub with a well-known jewellery fence. It could have something to do with his brother. We will speak to all parties tomorrow."

Grace looked tired. The evening had obviously taken its toll.

"I'm falling asleep," she admitted. "It's been a lovely evening but we'd better go. This pair has school tomorrow too."

Greco leaned forward and placed a kiss on her forehead. "I'll get your coats."

# Chapter 8

Nadia Pakulski was frantic. The two uniformed men had been at her front door for over thirty minutes, banging, ringing the bell, and calling her name. She had no idea who they were or what they wanted. Nadia had rung her husband, Vasili, but he was working and could do nothing. His command of English was no better than hers, so it was doubtful he'd be much use anyway. What Nadia needed was one of her teenage daughters.

She rang their school, East Manchester Academy. She didn't understand what the woman on the line was asking. Nadia kept repeating, *Zosia, Elena!* Her tone was urgent — surely the woman had to understand? Finally she heard her eldest daughter's voice.

"Elena, you must come home at once," Nadia shouted into the phone in Polish. "There are men at the door. They won't go away. They have paperwork. It looks official. They put a letter through the letterbox, but I don't know what it means. They bang and shout, and I am afraid."

"Don't let them in," Elena urged. "I think I know who they are. I have been expecting this. You and Papa have had these letters before. They are from the courts. I think Papa has been hiding them. The landlord wants us out. He gave us notice three months ago. I told Papa, but he said it would be okay. I think that is what the men want."

"They want to throw us out onto the streets?" Nadia was even more worried now. Where would they go? She knew no one who could help them.

"I'll come home. I'll speak to someone. It will be okay. Just don't let them in."

"Who will you speak to?"

"A young woman I know. She will help us. She has helped others in our situation. She will know what to do."

* * *

Elena Pakulski told her teacher that her mother was ill, and needed to go to a doctor. She explained that her mother didn't speak English well, so she would have to go with her. Mrs Pattison wasn't happy. But given the circumstances, Mrs Pattison had little choice but to let her go.

Elena knew exactly who to go to. She made for the community centre on the Lansdowne. It wasn't a place she went often. Her parents had warned her off. But there was someone there who would help her.

Elena had met Dee through her friend Maria. She lived in a block of flats on the estate and had done English lessons at the centre. On one occasion when Elena had gone to meet her friend, Maria had introduced her. Despite her unusual appearance, Dee was okay. Maria spoke well of her, told her how she helped people. Elena had no choice now but to trust her.

Dee was packing books away and tidying the room ready for the next group. Elena approached her and began to explain their problem.

"That bastard Barton wants to throw you out?" Dee said as Elena wiped tears from her eyes. "He doesn't get any better. It's about time someone sorted him once and for all."

"You know him?"

"I know his methods. He does his homework and always stays within the law. He'll have another family lined up willing to pay a lot more."

"We can pay more. My father works hard," Elena said.

"It doesn't work like that. You must have done something to upset him," Dee explained patiently. "Complained, for example."

"We wrote a letter. The place is so damp my sister Zosia coughs all night. It makes her chest bad." Elena was close to tears again. Despite her youth, her parents put a lot of responsibility on her young shoulders. If Dee couldn't help, she'd no idea who to try next.

Dee folded her arms. "That'll be it then. Barton doesn't do criticism. He doesn't do repairs either. He will get new tenants and start again."

"Surely, he can't do that. We pay the rent on time, we are good tenants. We have nowhere else to go. Please, you have to tell him. We won't complain anymore. My father will try to fix the place up. We have to stay. We cannot live on the streets."

"He gave you a lease? Did you read it?"

"Yes, I explained it to my parents and they thought it fair."

"Bet it wasn't for long, was it? About six months is usual for him. How long have you lived there?"

"Nearly one year."

"Did your parents get letters about this?"

"Yes. Papa put them in the drawer. He didn't read them."

"One of them will have been giving your parents notice to leave. In that case, you won't beat him. The man knows all the tricks. He has the law on his side. Your lease has expired and therefore he has the right to make you leave. The men at your door will be bailiffs. There is nothing you or your family can do. Barton holds all the cards. You will have to leave, today."

Elena's eyes widened. "Surely it won't come to that? We have nowhere to go. What will we do?"

"This hasn't just come out of the blue," said Dee. "The letters. If your parents couldn't read them, then they should have got help. Didn't they think to make plans?"

"They didn't realise how urgent the letters were. Mama can't read English, and Papa's isn't that good. Besides, he's always working."

"What does he do?"

"He drives a truck for a friend."

This sparked Dee's interest. "Does he ever drive to Europe? Use the ferries?" she asked.

"No, just local deliveries."

"That could still be useful. I'll try and sort this for you. I will speak to Barton on your behalf. I'll tell him you won't cause him any more trouble." She paused. "But there will be conditions. He may insist that your father works for a different firm from now on, one that Barton chooses. But be warned. He's not a nice man. Barton will make demands. He's as hard to work for as he is to have as a landlord."

"We'll do anything. Papa will. We just need a place to live. Somewhere we can live in peace."

* * *

"I've had a call from Dr Bowers at the Duggan," Greco told the team. "He is doing the PMs on the lads later."

Speedy shuddered. "Gruesome."

Greco had already decided not to take Grace with him. In her condition, the experience might be too much for her. "Then steel yourself, Sergeant, because you are coming with me."

"Can I have a word in your office?" Grace asked.

Greco led the way.

"I don't mind coming to the PM," Grace whispered. "Don't sideline me because of the baby."

"Whether you like it or not, we have to factor it in. I don't want you throwing up, so I'll take Speedy. I want you and Joel to go and find Max Marsh. Speak to him about the photo the lads sent him. Yesterday, he said he hadn't heard from them. Now we know that was a lie. He is holding back. I want to know why."

"Okay, but when do we tell that lot out there? It can't stay a secret for much longer. With you fussing around me, they are bound to get suspicious."

The prospect filled Greco with dread. "McCabe first, then we'll see." Grace went back to her desk.

Leah left her notes and went into Greco's office.

"I spoke to Bert Banister earlier," she told him. "He insists that what happened between him and Dave Holt last night was nothing more serious than the drink. Holt had had a skinful, and they got into the ruck about football."

"He's lying."

"I know, sir, but what can we do? He insists Holt didn't hit him, and even if he had, Banister won't press charges.

"There is something going on there. I suspect that Dave Holt was trying to sell some jewellery. Keep an eye on that pub. Do you have anyone in there?"

"You mean like Roman?" She smiled. Greco knew that Roman was Leah's informant, who'd proved very useful in the past.

"I'll go and find him later and have a word with him anyway. For a little extra he might switch venues for a week or two," she said

Greco nodded. They certainly needed a break. They had no positive motive for the two killings. They presumed it had something to do with stealing, or finding the packets at Ava Whitton's house. But that was nothing more than conjecture. They weren't even sure it was the house the lads had gone to.

He called through to the main office. "Joel? Do a trawl of that road Ava Whitton lives on. Gather up any CCTV from private cameras the other residents might have."

# Chapter 9

Dr Bob Bowers stood between the two bodies. "A thorough job was done on the pair of them," he told Greco and Speedy. "DNA evidence has confirmed their identities and there are no surprises. They are Holt and Riley. This one, Vinny Holt, died from severe head injuries."

"Not from being set alight?" Speedy asked.

Dr Bowers looked up at the two detectives standing on the viewing platform. "No, there is no soot deposit in his airway. Same with Craig Riley. Both lads were dead before they were set alight. Both died from blows to the head. Then, it seems, the fun started. Though I can't for the life of me work out why."

"What do you mean?" asked Greco.

"The violence perpetrated on both bodies after death was excessive. Take Vinny Holt. The fingers on the lad's right hand were cut off and stuffed down his throat one at a time. A neat job, longest one first followed by the index finger, then the other two and finally the thumb."

Speedy gasped. "Poor bugger!"

"He was already dead, Sergeant, remember? Jammed in tight they were. I have recovered them and found something of interest. More about that later. Craig Riley's fingers were also hacked off. All we have are charred remains, I'm afraid. The bodies were set alight and an attempt was also made to burn the body parts. We found fingers, an eye and part of a foot in the plastic bag."

Greco heard Speedy inhale sharply. "Thank God the poor buggers were dead," he whispered to his DCI.

"Yes, it looked at first like they had been tortured, but the mutilations occurred post-mortem. All the body parts were hacked off crudely — with speed I'd say — burnt and left with the bodies. There is nothing missing. It was then that the bodies were laid into with something heavy and metal. Both bodies have extensive broken bones."

"And still they were set on fire, even after all that?" Greco asked.

Dr Bowers nodded. "Rather excessive, I grant you. With regard to Riley, I have recovered flecks of rust embedded in his back. He was on his back when found, so the fire damage was not so extensive. The metal object used was definitely not new."

"And you're absolutely sure they were dead before all this was done to them?" Speedy asked.

Bob Bowers looked at him and smiled. The sergeant was looking distinctly green around the gills.

"Yes, Sergeant. No doubt about it."

Greco shuddered. "Is there any forensic evidence apart from the rust?"

"Not yet, but tests are ongoing. They were found naked, so there's no clothing to look at. Plus, the fire destroyed most of what we might have got from the bodies. We have taken skin swabs, fibres and other debris from their hair. Both Holt and Riley's DNA is on record. So formalising identity won't be a problem."

That was small compensation. There was no way Greco wanted the families involved in any sort of ID procedure. What they'd see was just too horrific.

"Roxy will do her best with the samples she is testing. You never know. But my guess is we won't get much. Whoever did this was good at the job. I have seen this sort of brutality before in cases where the poor unfortunate was used as a warning to others. But on those occasions the victim was usually still alive while the beating and abuse took place."

"If drug dealing is involved, sir, that would make sense," Speedy noted.

What Greco didn't understand was, why kill them first and then make it look as if they had been beaten and tortured? They desperately needed to know what these lads had taken from that house, and what those packages contained. But more to the point, they needed to know the name of who'd done this. Somehow Greco didn't think it was Ava Whitton.

"Any sign of drugs?" Greco asked the doctor.

"Blood tests show that both of them were sedated."

Greco nodded. "What was used?"

"As I said, Roxy is still doing tests. She also took swabs from under their fingernails. We found a faint trace of heroin on Vinny Holt's index finger. Speaking of which, Professor Batho would like a word before you leave. That something of interest I mentioned earlier."

Speedy nudged Greco. "Wonder what nuggets of wisdom he wants to add."

"We need all the help we can get," Greco said.

Julian Batho wasn't to everyone's taste. Speedy found him hard going. And he was. But Greco understood the professor. They had suffered a similar experience. Both had lost the woman they loved in tragic circumstances. Julian didn't suffer fools either. Like Greco, he took his work seriously.

"Heroin, you say. Maybe that was what was in the packets."

Speedy nodded. "It would make sense. A valuable haul. You can understand why the killer would want it back."

Moments later, Julian joined them. "Come along to the adjoining room, gentlemen. There is someone I'd like you to meet."

Greco was intrigued. There was a slight smile on the professor's lips. Did that mean the blackness was lifting? After what happened to Imogen Goode, Julian had been in the depths of depression for months.

"Hope it's not another bloody body. Got enough on with this little lot," Speedy grumbled.

"Whatever or whoever it is, Julian obviously thinks it's important to our case," Greco said.

The room next door was another post-mortem lab. It was a relief to see an empty table. Then Julian led them to the fridge and pulled out one of the drawers.

"I'd like you to meet 'Festival Fred,'" he said with relish. "So named because he was found at the site of that big music festival in south Cheshire last summer."

Speedy took a step back. It was a body, or what was left of one. "God, what a mess!" The skin looked like seasoned black leather that had been glued to the skeleton. "What happened to the poor bugger?"

"Badly beaten. His skull is cracked, so the head wound could have killed him. We can't be sure. Not content with that, the perpetrator set the body on fire." Julian's tone was matter of fact. "Fred's case is in the hands of the Cheshire police, but they need the input of expert forensics. Hence, he's here with us. Of course, we don't know if the violence was perpetrated before or after death. Has Dr Bowers told you about the rings?"

Greco smiled. "No, I think he was leaving the good stuff to you."

"Vinny Holt had a ring on his little finger. Dr Bowers recovered it when he removed the digit. Festival Fred was wearing an identical ring, also recovered from a finger we found in roughly this area." Julian pointed to Fred's throat. "It was the same style, quite distinctive, and had the same hallmark on the inside. Both were initialled, but the letters are well worn. I will work on them some more. The rings are gold but were not assayed in the UK. The hallmark is small but we have narrowed it down to one of two possibilities. Fred's killing is remarkably similar to those of the young men in there." Julian nodded to the next room.

"Are you suggesting that this individual knew Vinny?" Greco asked.

"That one is for you, but it is probable that they both met your killer."

"Had Fred been beaten and his body mutilated?" asked Greco.

"It is difficult to ascertain from the remains. But there are broken bones, and the finger is significant."

"It is possible that Vinny stole that ring."

"Yes. We are testing for prints, but it will be tricky. Fred's ring had obviously been on his finger for years. It must have been an extremely tight fit. It had worn a faint mark on the bone. Had there been any flesh on the bone, a distinct groove would have been visible. I have no idea where Holt got his from or how long he'd had it."

It struck Greco that it might have been part of the haul from Ava Whitton's house — if there had been a robbery. "How long has this one been dead?" asked Greco.

"Difficult to say. We're still doing tests. Fred was found in a ditch, in a Cheshire field last summer. It is probable that he had been buried there. The soil in the ditch was peaty, and it was waterlogged for much of the time. It aided preservation to some extent. We are looking at stomach contents, insect life, and plant pollens found on him in an effort to determine when he died and where."

"Do you have his clothing?"

"No, Inspector. Like Riley and Holt, he was naked. But he had been placed in a black plastic bag."

"If he was found in water, how come you are looking for pollen?" Speedy asked.

"It is lodged in his hair, ears and nose. So far we have found rape seed and sugar-beet pollen. That suggests a farming area. Perhaps somewhere like East Anglia, for example."

"What do you know about him?" asked Greco.

"Male, about thirty years, and undernourished. His last meal was bread and water, which suggests that perhaps he was being kept prisoner somewhere. He's had a knee injury that at some time required surgery. He had an allergy to peanuts. And it is highly likely he was Polish."

That was a lot of information. Greco was rightly impressed. But it was worth nothing without solid evidence to back it up.

"And just how did you deduce that?"

"He was wearing one of those medical-alert bracelets on his wrist, Inspector. The words can just be made out on the medallion and they're written in Polish. Plus, Roxy traced the maker's mark on the ring to a jeweller in Warsaw."

# Chapter 10

They made their way out of the morgue. Looking thoughtful, Speedy said, "Perhaps we should have a word with the couple who found Fred."

"We'll see," Greco said. "First, we'll have a look at the statement the pair gave, and we'll go from there. Given he was buried a while before the festival, I doubt they had anything to do with it."

"What now, guv?"

"We'll check out those rings. The photos are on the system. A job for you when we get back to the station. We need the maker's name, and who they were made for. Initials aren't much good on their own. We need names, addresses, you know the drill."

Speedy shrugged. "Maybe they were sold in every jewellery shop in Warsaw."

"They were expensive pieces and initialled. The jeweller who made them will have records."

"Ava Whitton does have Wi-Fi, I checked. I've asked for her internet history from the provider."

"Anything known?" asked Greco.

"She has no online presence, but she must use it for something."

"I'm more interested in the friends she has, her family and if she gets on with the neighbours. What job she does and how she fits in. Work on the small details, Sergeant."

Suddenly Speedy turned to him and said, "Does Grace seem a bit off to you?"

The questions were starting. Folk noticing that Grace was not quite her usual self. Greco cleared his throat. "Seems okay to me."

"She's not. There's something, but she's not saying. I've known Grace a while, remember? I can spot the signs."

"Perhaps it would be better to keep out of it. Go nosing around her private life and Grace won't thank you for it," Greco warned him.

"I mention it because I think it has something to do with work." Speedy paused. "Grace isn't looking for another post somewhere else, is she, guv?"

"Not that I'm aware of. What makes you think that?"

"She's been late a few times. Goes missing with no explanation. I wondered if she'd been going to job interviews."

Greco shook his head. He almost smiled. "If that were the case, I'm sure she'd have told me."

* * *

Grace and Joel walked into the community centre. The place was full. A group of older teens, crowded around Graham Clovelly, began to whisper as soon as they spotted the detectives. Max Marsh was in his room with a group of pensioners. The café was busy with mums and tots.

Graham hurried across to greet them. He spoke in an undertone. "I hope this is important. It's taken a while to gain this lot's trust. Keep turning up like this and you'll scare them off. I don't fancy going through the whole uphill struggle again. So if you speak to anyone, just go easy, will you?"

"We haven't come here just to make people nervous. We're investigating two murders," Grace reminded him. "We need to speak to Max Marsh again."

"You have to see it from my point of view," Graham said apologetically. "I don't want any trouble. The lads you see over there are in my pool group, and moving up the rankings. A couple of them are 'angels.' The realisation that they are good at something and are an asset to the community has given them their self-esteem back. They've all got history with you lot. Some of them get argumentative at the drop of a hat. But being part of this centre, coming here and taking part in the tournaments, it's paying dividends out there on the streets." He looked at Joel. "You know what I mean?"

Joel nodded. "We're not here to stir things up, Graham. A quick word with Max in there, and we're off."

"Okay, but tread carefully. He's with the seniors. I don't want them upsetting either. Do I call him out?"

"No, it's okay," Grace said. "We'll go in and take a look at what's going on."

There were tables all around the circumference of the room. Each had one or two people sitting at laptops and working on an exercise.

Marsh looked at the detectives and frowned. "I'm busy."

"A quick word. We won't keep you." Grace smiled. She'd recognised one of the group members, a woman who lived on her street. She waved at her.

"What's he been up to, love?" the woman called to Grace.

Grace shook her head. "Nothing, Doreen. We want a quick word, that's all."

"I heard about the lads. It's been on the news. Nasty. Makes you afraid to go out at nights."

"I'm sure you're quite alright." Grace smiled again.

Marsh interrupted. "We're in the middle of something. Some of them need a lot of help, so make it quick."

"We're here about the text you got from Vinny Holt," Grace said. "The one with the picture of the house. Why didn't you say something to my colleagues yesterday?"

He shrugged. "I forgot. Anyway, it was nothing important, just a house."

"We'll be the judge of that. Can I see it?"

"Look, I don't have time for this."

"We can always take you down to the station, Mr Marsh. You'll have plenty of time there."

Marsh gave her a filthy look.

"So, what's it to be?"

Marsh took his mobile from the back pocket of his jeans and handed it to her. "Nothing to hide. Look all you want."

Grace flipped through the texts until she found the one from Vinny. The word 'house,' plus the picture. "You really should have shown this to my colleagues," she told him.

"Take it with you. Do whatever tests you want. I've got nothing to hide. I've no idea why Vinny sent that to me. I never saw him again, so I couldn't ask him."

Grace made a note of the date and time it was sent. "Do you mind if I forward the text to my own phone?"

Marsh shrugged. "Like I said, do what you want."

Once she'd finished, Grace handed the phone back. "That's fine. One more thing. Do you recognise the house?"

"No, and I've no idea who lives there either."

"Thanks for your time," she said. Turning to Doreen, she called out, "Take care!"

They left the room. "We'll get his phone history when we get back. You never know," Joel said. "He's hiding something, I just feel it."

Doreen followed them out into the café. She spoke quietly to Grace. "Have you come about the thieving? I didn't report it. I left that to Graham, but it's still going on."

Grace was taken aback. They moved out of earshot of the others. "You're telling me that things are going missing?"

"It's been happening for a while. I had a gold watch taken, it belonged to my husband. Others have had bits and pieces disappear. Joe even had money taken from his bank account."

They had been given the impression that Graham Clovelly had turned the place around, and that the youngsters were fast becoming a reformed bunch. Thieving wasn't on Grace's radar. "Does he want to talk to us about it?"

"He doesn't want any trouble. It was only a tenner, but like I told him, that's not the point. It meant that someone had got into his online bank account. I think he had a word with his bank. They'll probably have sorted it."

"If you haven't done so already, you should tell Graham again, and say you've spoken to me. If you want to talk some more, particularly if no one does anything this time, here's my card."

"Graham won't want to involve the police. Very protective of his lads, he is."

"Thieving is thieving, Doreen. Someone has to take action and make it stop."

"What's he done anyway?" Doreen nodded back at Marsh.

"Nothing. He's simply being helpful." Grace smiled.

"Trouble is, I'm not sure who he's helping," she whispered to Joel on their way out.

\* \* \*

"Vinny Holt did send Max Marsh a photo of Ava Whitton's house," Joel told the team.

Greco made a note of it on the incident board. He'd called a briefing to collate what they had gleaned so far. Which, apart from the photo, wasn't much.

"The visit did throw up something else," Grace said. "There is some petty thieving going on at the centre. Probably got nothing to do with our case though."

"What sort of thieving?" Greco asked.

"A watch, stuff like that. One elderly man had money taken from his bank account."

Greco frowned. "The way things are, we don't know if it's significant or not. Because of Dave Holt's recent association with Banister, we suspect that jewellery might have been taken from Ava Whitton's place. Go back, get descriptions, and we'll circulate them. As for the money, the pensioners are learning how to use computers. It might just be a mistake, but have a word with the gentleman, and tell uniform."

"I have been researching the maker's mark on the two rings," Leah told them. "The shop no longer exists. However, the son of the original jeweller moved to the UK about five years ago. We need to find him. See what records he has retained or can put his hands on."

Speedy sounded doubtful. "If he's moved here permanently it's unlikely he can help much, if at all. He's not going to have brought his business records with him."

Greco sighed. "There was the trace of a name engraved on the inside of Festival Fred's ring. Julian will do his best. He should have something for us soon."

Speedy had a point about the records, but it didn't help. What they badly needed was a motive for the two murders. Simply suspecting that the murdered lads may have seen, or stolen heroin from Ava Whitton's house wasn't enough. They had to know for sure.

# Chapter 11

Day 4

Ava Whitton was not going into work this morning. She had more important things to do. Barton wanted a meeting. Damn the man, he'd had the cheek to take her to task about the robbery at her house. Ava would have to watch her step. He was more than capable of doing her harm. Despite the good clothes and the charm, he was a thug who hurt people. Her eyes drifted to the inside of her right arm and a nasty scar — Barton's work. He'd cut her in punishment for a late delivery. In the early days of their relationship, he had shown little tolerance. Nowadays, things were thankfully easier. They had reached the stage in the relationship where his need for her was greater than hers for him, but Ava still didn't trust him. She disliked the man intensely. She wanted out.

There had been twenty-four packets in the fridge. For reasons best known to themselves, the lads who robbed her had left six behind. On a more personal front, not only had they taken the drugs, but money and jewellery too. The jewellery was irreplaceable, family pieces.

They had forced the lock on a downstairs window at the back. There was hardly any mess, just a length of bent plastic where they'd jemmied the double-glazed frame away from the lock. But Barton would not be interested in that kind of detail. He'd blame her lax security, and try to make her pay. Ava knew she had to find a way to placate him. It required just the right touch. If she was too apologetic about what had happened, he'd take advantage. Barton had to believe that Ava was as outraged about the robbery as he was. But more importantly, he must not find out that she still had some of the heroin.

The meet up was scheduled for ten that morning in a coffee shop on the High Street in Manchester city centre. Barton had wanted a venue busy enough for both of them to go unnoticed. But that didn't suit Ava. Just in case anything went wrong, she wanted people to recall seeing her. She wore a deep red, fitted, knee-length dress and a black jacket. Her shoes and matching bag were red leather. She was tall, upright and definitely not dressed to blend in, despite what Barton wanted. And it worked. Eyes turned her way as she entered the coffee shop.

Barton was a big man, broad and muscular with closely cropped dark hair. His coarse features were clean shaven and he was dressed as usual in a suit with a white shirt and tie. The acceptable face of his grubby little business. But Ava knew very well that this was not a true picture of the man. His persona was every bit as false as her own. Barton was a conman and a crook. But worse than that, he was a very successful drug trafficker. And that was why he needed her. In a short space of time, Ava had become a vital cog in his illicit enterprise.

He sat at a window table. He looked her up and down, then nodded a cursory greeting. "I already have a coffee. You get your own."

Ava ignored this and sat down. Barton was not someone she'd choose to chat to over a mid-morning drink. He had once been a necessary evil, but now it was time to get out. One way or another, this had to be wound up. Meanwhile, she would be polite, businesslike, and pray it did the trick.

"We have a problem. Thanks to you," he hissed. His face was hard. There were deep lines down both cheeks as if they'd been etched in stone. "I have missing merchandise. My customers are not happy. They do not expect to be short changed."

Barton's demeanour expressed an anger that, despite the suit, he couldn't hide. He could inflict a great deal of damage with a single punch. No one crossed him twice. Ava was well aware of the risk she was taking.

"You expect me to believe that, after what you did to those boys?"

"I am missing an entire shipment. Those boys stole it from your house, Ava. Convenient, don't you think? You moved the goods to a place where they could get their thieving hands on it. For your sake, I hope that was not deliberate. You wouldn't try to double-cross me, would you? Because if you steal from me and it backfires, I will retaliate." He gave her an oily smile. "So, I will give you a choice. You either give my goods back, or pay me the full street price."

Both those options were impossible. Ava's stomach was churning. This was worse than she had expected. Barton believed that she had played some part in the theft. "You know that can't be done. I don't have that sort of money. And you are wrong, I didn't have anything to do with the theft of your goods. I lost things too, things precious to me."

"And my customers, Ava, the dealers I supply? What do I tell them? They are not nice people. Perhaps I should tell them about you, eh? Let your name slip. I wonder how long it would be before you were found dead in a ditch!"

"I have told you. It was not down to me! I didn't know this would happen." Ava took a deep breath. "Just this once, your customers will have to accept it. Give them a refund." Ava's tone was even, and she looked him full in the face. She watched his expression change. He was trying hard to keep his temper in check, aware of the people all around.

"I don't think you understand, Ava. My customers are not the 'accepting' type. They order, they pay and they expect to receive the goods. Half-arsed excuses do not go down well."

He brought his face close to hers and spoke the words slowly. His foul breath turned Ava's stomach.

"It is not an excuse, you moron!" she snapped back. She showed anger, but inside she was quaking with fear. She recoiled slightly. "We had Customs and Excise poking around at work. I had to think quick. What was I supposed to do — let them find the stuff?" Now she leaned forward too, and whispered, "You forget, it is me who takes the risks. The driver brought the goods to the depot. They are told not to, but it was late. He had been on the road for hours. It was his intention to move it the following morning. I had no choice, I had to take the stuff home or risk it being discovered. Be assured, Barton, if that had happened, I would not have protected you!"

"Ungrateful bitch!" he sneered. "Without me you would still be scraping a living, selling your scrawny body on street corners like before. Think about it, Ava. I got you the fancy job in that smart office. I pay you well for your part in my little enterprise. But you show me nothing but disrespect. You need teaching a lesson!"

"It is me who takes the flak if things go wrong, Barton," she shot back angrily. "You do nothing but sit back and wait for the shipments to arrive."

"Do not deviate from the plan again," he warned. "Your drivers do as they are told. They deliver before they arrive at your depot. They know the drill well enough. It is up to you to ensure they keep to the rules. And don't forget, you owe me. You will get nothing until I have recouped the money from the missing stuff. I will deduct the amount from your next payments."

He expected her to take risks and work for nothing, did he? "Do that and we are through." Ava spoke the words slowly, deliberately, and she meant them. Yes, she was afraid, but he would not dictate to her any more. During the time she'd worked for Barton, Ava had salted away enough money to live off for the rest of her life. She could disappear. She would ensure that no one came looking for her. No one would ask questions.

"The police have been to my house," she hissed at him. "They are suspicious. Perhaps I should tell them the truth. Protect myself."

"You won't do that. The risk to yourself is too great." His smile was icy. "Cross me, Ava, and I will hunt you down and kill you with my bare hands. I also know that the thieves didn't take all of the gear. You will return the remaining packets to me."

Ava was taken aback. Where had he got that information from? There could only be one source. The two butchered lads themselves. "How do you know that?" she asked, her voice shaking.

"Because I have people on my payroll who earn their crust. Unlike some." Barton's eyes narrowed. "It is safe, I hope?"

Ava didn't reply.

"You will deliver it to my lock-up tonight."

"No." She was adamant. "The remainder of that shipment is my insurance. I read the papers. You killed those boys. You butchered them like you did my brother!" The words brought tears to her eyes. Tomasz had worked for Barton too at one time. Then, without explanation, he had disappeared, never to be heard from again. "You are a cold-blooded killer. I have to ensure my own safety. I have no other choice."

Barton's face was thunderous. "Be warned, Ava. Don't cross me. Give me back what is mine or you will die," he hissed.

Without another word, he stood up and stormed out of the café.

Ava felt sick. Had she gone too far? Barton knew only one way to sort those who disobeyed him. She had to do something, make herself safe. She noticed a young man clearing the tables and she beckoned him over.

"That man who just left. I think he stole my purse." At first the young man seemed unsure of what to do. Ava was searching in her bag. "He distracted me. He must have taken it while my back was turned."

"I'll get the manager."

He rushed off and returned with an older man in tow.

"You're sure?" the manager asked. "You haven't put it somewhere?"

"No!" Ava wailed. "It was on the table. He just got up and left suddenly. He has to have taken it."

"Okay, I'll ring the police. There is CCTV outside on the adjoining shop. They will have got a good image of the man."

Ava nodded, and smiled gratefully. This was good. Police interest in Barton would get him off her back long enough for her to formulate a plan.

\* \* \*

Barton was angry. Ava had outfoxed him. He wanted to get even, but he also wanted his heroin back. He fed a large distribution network and that missing shipment would give him a problem, leading to lost income and angry customers. For now, he would play Ava's game. But he had already made up his mind that she had outlived her usefulness. He would not allow anyone to dictate the rules of the game. It was his operation, and always had been.

His mobile rang. It was the young woman. They had never met, but he knew her history, who she was, and how to find her if necessary. She had proved to be a useful pair of eyes and ears. She had told one of his people about the heroin left behind at Ava's. As a rule, they conducted business entirely over the phone. But perhaps the time had come to meet her. She knew what was going on locally, and it occurred to him that she might be a suitable replacement for Ava. Barton decided to set that up as soon as possible.

"The Pakulski family will play ball," she told him. "The father has an HGV licence. Do you want to see him?"

"No. Send him to see Ms Whitton at Greyson Logistics. She will set things up."

"Will you call off the bailiffs? Do I tell his family they can stay in the house?"

"Yes, but I don't want to hear another word about the damp, and the rent will be going up."

"Thanks. They'll be pleased."

"I want us to meet. I'll text you the place. Don't let me down."

# Chapter 12

Greco addressed the team. "The community centre has recently become the hub of that estate, particularly for the young folk. All down to the efforts of that do-gooder, Clovelly. Despite the change of attitude and behaviour, I don't believe that the youngsters who use the place weren't aware of what Craig and Vinny were up to. We will speak to them again. Get Clovelly on side."

"I'll have a word, sir," Joel volunteered. "Graham has done an excellent job of straightening out some of the lads. But I agree, if Craig and Vinny were planning something, the centre is where they'd talk about it. Max Marsh knows more than he's told us, has to. Otherwise why was he sent the photo?"

"Vinny Holt went home with money. Then he went out again. Craig did much the same. Where did they go? The centre? The Grapes? We need to know, and then we can attempt to track them from there. We should talk to Callum Riley too. Him and Craig were brothers, they were bound to share things." Greco looked at Joel and Speedy. "Get out there and ask questions. Also, do we have the footage from the road Ava Whitton lives on?"

"Only one of her neighbours has a camera, sir," Joel told them. "The quality of the film isn't good. They have it positioned in front of a tall hedge. It does a good job of capturing what's going on in their own garden and drive, but it gets nothing else."

"Not even a shot of the road?"

Joel shook his head. "No, sir."

"In that case, we will ask forensics to take a look inside her property. If we're lucky, they might find a fingerprint or trace of heroin."

"How do we square that one?" Speedy asked. "We have nothing. We're not sure the lads were even there."

"We now have the photo from Marsh. I will speak to Ava Whitton. Given what has happened, she had better have a good reason to refuse."

"While I was in the area, I asked the neighbours about her," Joel said. "She doesn't mix, and apart from tradesmen, no one ever goes to the house. She lives alone and has no pets. She bought the house new two years ago. She paid cash and didn't sell a property in order to buy the one in Handforth."

"Do we know how long she's been working at Greysons?"

"Five years, sir."

"Their personnel department will have her previous address. Get it, will you?"

Just then a uniformed officer entered the room and beckoned to Greco. "This could be important, sir. It's Dave Holt. He's been picked up in the Ashtree pub in Gorton again. This time he wasn't just talking about selling jewellery, he had stuff on him. A stroke of luck for us — the bloke he was selling to was being watched. A separate case another team are working on. We brought him here because he's connected to the murders you're currently investigating."

Greco turned to the team. "You all heard that?"

They nodded.

"Speedy, you and I will speak to him." Greco turned back to the officer. "Did you recover the jewellery?"

"Yes, we did. Quite a haul."

"We'll take a look first. Grace, get that list and descriptions from the centre." He beckoned for Speedy to follow him.

The jewellery was laid out on a table in the evidence room. Some of it was cheap fashion jewellery, but there were one or two pieces that looked valuable. Among them was a gold watch. It was old-fashioned and had the name 'Joe Davies' engraved on the back.

Speedy peered at it. "What's the betting this belongs to one of the seniors that use that centre?"

But Greco's attention was elsewhere. He'd picked up a locket. It had a heavy gold chain, and the locket itself had 'Ava' inscribed on the back. "It looks like this belongs to Ava Whitton. If so, then the two lads have to have taken it from her house." He smiled. "There is stuff here stolen from the centre and from Ava's house. That means the lads must have been involved in both. It needs investigating, and Max Marsh is our best bet there. As far as we know, the thefts were all from folk in his group."

"Do you reckon he's involved too, sir?"

"Very possibly. But with regard to Ava, this is our way in." He passed the locket to Speedy. "We now have a legitimate reason to send in forensics. She can hardly complain, can she?"

"There is a maker's mark on here too, sir. I'll check it out, but it looks like the ones on the rings."

"The locket is old and valuable. Open it up," Greco told Speedy.

It was a fiddly thing and obviously hadn't been opened for years. Speedy held it out to Greco in the palm of his hand. "There's a lock of hair inside. What d'you make of that, sir?"

"At a guess, I'd say it was infant's hair. If it does belong to Ava, she'll want it back."

\* \* \*

Speedy left Greco and went to look in on Dave Holt. He stood outside for a few moments, watching the man pace the cell floor. He'd been apprehended while attempting to sell the gold watch to a local villain, Bert Banister — the bloke he'd attacked. They had both been apprehended at the very moment the money changed hands.

"Have him brought along to interview room three," he told the desk sergeant.

Speedy and Greco interviewed him together.

Dave Holt wasn't having any. He kept insisting he was innocent. "That watch was my grandad's. He left it to my mum, but she'll never wear it. We need the money. We've got a funeral to pay for, you know. Forgotten that, have you?" He leant forward in his chair. "Bloody coppers. Pounced on me like I was vermin. Everyone was watching. It's my local too."

"Come on, Dave. This never belonged to a member of your family." Speedy looked closely at it. The watch bracelet was all solid gold links. "This will have cost a fortune. Tell me the truth. It's got something to do with your Vinny and what he was mixed up in, hasn't it?"

"No! You're wrong. The lad wasn't involved in 'owt. And you can't prove otherwise. This stuff is my mother's. So unless you've got evidence to prove me wrong, I want out of here."

"Do you want a solicitor?" asked Greco.

"No, I don't intend stopping long."

"Then tell us the truth. Where did you get the watch?" Greco said patiently. "This isn't just about robbery. As you well know, we are investigating two murders. One of them is your own brother. Do you know anything about those, Dave?"

Dave looked horrified. "You can't pin those killings on me! I'm innocent. I might have given our kid a clip around the ear occasionally, but I'd never hurt him for real."

"The watch. Where did it come from?" Greco persisted. "We know it isn't yours. Very soon the real owner will come and identify it. Lying to us is a waste of your time and ours."

Dave Holt's face fell. He sighed. "Okay, I'll tell you what I know. But it goes against the grain, copper. I don't grass, not on my own brother!"

"I think Vinny would understand," Greco said. "He'd certainly want us to catch whoever killed him."

"Vinny got home that day right full of himself. Like I told you, he bunged mum fifty and then got ready to go out. He was meeting Craig. The pair of them planned to hit town. There was a gig on in some pub in Manchester. They were going to get a taxi. We had a bit of banter about the cost, but Vinny wasn't having any. Said he had a bob or two, and to keep my nose out. After he left, I had a look round his room. I found the jewellery and a bundle of notes stashed in the bottom of his wardrobe."

"You should have told us before. That would've saved a lot of legwork." Speedy said. "Did you ask him where he got it from?"

"Never got the chance, did I? Next thing I knew, he'd been done in. I took the money, spent some, and then panicked. I know what it looks like, but I didn't hurt those lads."

"Do you know anything about the heroin?" Greco asked.

"Heroin?" Dave Holt looked genuinely puzzled. "There was no heroin, just dosh and jewellery."

"Don't lie to us again, Dave." Speedy leaned forward and gave him a look full of menace. "Feed us more lies and we'll throw the bloody book at you!"

"It's not a lie. That is all there was."

"If we presume that Craig Riley took his share, what would he have done with it?" Greco asked.

"Much the same as Vinny. Although Craig wouldn't want his mother or Callum rooting around in his stuff. Up until the killings, there was just the twins and her at home. She's a right nosey cow. Vinny told me once that Craig stashed stuff under a loose floorboard in his bedroom."

# Chapter 13

The man who stood in front of Ava Whitton was in his fifties, thin and small with dark hair. His clothes had seen better days, but he looked reasonably tidy, and he was clean shaven. In any event, she had little choice. Barton had sent him to her. As far as that thug was concerned, everything had to seem normal. They were standing outside in the huge yard belonging to Greyson Logistics. Half a dozen lorries were parked up against the far wall.

"You will have to learn better English, Vasili," Ava told him. She looked at the teenage girl who'd accompanied him. "You must make him understand. Speaking good English is not an option, it's a necessity. How does he cope at the moment? You tell me he drives for a living. How does he read the road signs?"

"He uses a Polish satnav," Zosia Pakulski replied simply. "My father is a good man and a hard worker. He won't let you down."

"That is not in question. I can see that he is keen, but that is not enough. There are times when this job can get tricky. Sometimes our drivers are stopped by customs at the ferry ports, Calais or Dover. A soft touch is required. It helps if a driver is able to communicate well." That was putting it mildly. A smooth tongue and a friendly smile could work wonders in certain circumstances.

"Please give him a chance. Me and my sister Elena will help him. I have time off school soon. I can go with him."

Ava shook her head. "That would pose all sorts of problems, insurance and such."

"He needs the job. Being able to stay in our house depends on it," Zosia pleaded. "My sister spoke to a friend of hers who helps out at the community centre on the estate. She sent us to see you. We were told you would give Papa a job."

Ava looked a little closer at the girl. She was talking about someone who must know Barton, a girl Ava knew nothing about. "What is her name?"

"I only know her as Dee," Zosia replied.

Ava nodded. She had no choice. This man would be taken on. Officially, he would work for Greysons, but he was in hock to Barton just as much as she was. Eventually he would drive the firm's lorries across to Europe and back with cargo for bona fide customers, and drugs for Barton to distribute to his network.

"You will accompany George over there for now." Ava nodded at a middle-aged man sorting the cab in one of the lorries. "His next trip is in a couple of days, to Warsaw. He will give you the details. Speak to him and then go home and pack what you need. George will ring and tell you when to return. You will be gone for the better part of the coming week. Be aware that life as a long-distance driver is no picnic. You will be on the road for hours, eat in roadside cafes, and sleep in the cab, mostly in laybys along the route." Ava was wasting her time. The man didn't understand a word of what she said. She could have spoken to him in his native tongue, but she didn't want to do that at work. She nodded at Zosia. "Explain it to him, will you?"

"He is fine with that," the girl assured her.

"Another driver?" Martin Greyson was standing at the main entrance, watching her.

"We need him, Martin. Drivers don't stay long. We work them too hard."

"They don't complain," he retorted.

"Not to you. They daren't, Martin. You put the fear of God into most of them."

"That one is foreign."

"Most of them are," Ava replied. "Might not be so great when they drive the British roads, but it can be useful once they're in Europe. That one is Polish. He will go on the next run to Warsaw with George." She flashed him a rare smile and went back into the office building.

\* \* \*

Craig Riley's mother lived on the second floor of Trojan House on the Lansdowne. After what Dave Holt had told them, Greco had no difficulty in obtaining a search warrant for her flat.

"We go carefully. I don't want the woman upsetting," Greco told Speedy, who wasn't known for his tact. "She has just lost her son, remember. Whatever Craig took home and hid under the floorboards, it's unlikely his mother knows anything about it."

"What about the brother? D'you reckon he was in on this?"

"I've no idea, but we will question him. They were twins, lived under the same roof. Callum is bound to know things, whether he realises their importance or not."

Greco was right about Craig's mum. Joan Riley had no idea what they were on about, or why they would want to search her son's bedroom. However, with a warrant in place, she realised there was no choice.

"Is Callum here?" Greco asked.

"No, love, I've sent him to the supermarket. He won't be long though." She followed them into Craig's bedroom.

"He was a good lad mostly, our Craig, but he could give me grief too. Got himself into bother a few times, but not recently. Him and Vinny seemed to have turned a corner. Joined that group Clovelly runs. Became a pair of do-gooders. It changed the pair of them. Like I said before, Craig had even got himself an interview, a driving job with a firm in town."

"Which firm, Mrs Riley?" Greco asked.

"Greyson Logistics. They were going to train him up and everything."

"Guv," Speedy whispered. "That firm. It's where Ava Whitton works. She's the transport manager."

Greco hadn't forgotten. It might be important. They'd have to see. But the mention of that woman's name made him more determined than ever to search her house. Craig applies for a job, gets an interview and then robs the woman.

"Were your two boys close, Mrs Riley?" Greco asked.

"Not recently. Identical twins they might be, but they had very different personalities. Callum is kind and thoughtful. There's no way he'd get involved in the antics Craig did."

The lad sounded almost too good to be true.

"Found his stash!" Speedy announced with a smile. He'd moved the bed and lifted the loose floorboard. It was exactly as Dave Holt had told them. There was a roll of notes, mostly twenties, and a few items of jewellery. "No drugs or packets here. If they took any, the lads must have hidden them somewhere else."

\* \* \*

The items of jewellery were bagged up individually, ready for forensics. Before it was sent off, Greco decided to see how much of it had come from the community centre. The watch they knew about, but what about the rest?

Grace and Joel laid out the jewellery on one of the tables in Max Marsh's room. Each piece was in a clear plastic bag, so all folk had to do was take a look and point. Joel was ready with his notebook.

Graham shook his head in disbelief. "I don't believe this. It must have been going on for weeks, and right in front of my nose too."

"Like you say, going on for a while," Grace told him. "We need to find out who was involved in this. Craig and Vinny we know about, but there could be others. It was organised, they had a system. What we have to do now is find out who and how."

Clovelly addressed the group of pensioners. "Come and have a look. See if you recognise anything of yours."

"But don't touch," Grace added. "Just point it out to us and we'll get your names. You'll get it all back shortly. First, we need to check for fingerprints and the like."

The group was in sombre mood. Some of them had discussed the problem among themselves, but none had made a formal complaint. Max Marsh hung back. He stood by a window watching events.

"We didn't want to make a fuss," Doreen told Grace. "Graham does such a lot. None of us wanted to see him get into trouble. Or even worse, see this place close."

Grace smiled reassuringly at her. She pointed to the watch. "There is a gold watch. Was it yours?"

"Yes, love," Doreen replied and picked up the bag. "It's been missing for a month now. I'm so grateful to you for finding it. I thought I'd never get it back."

Grace took her to one side. "Who knew about your valuables?"

"No one but me. I keep this in a box in the sideboard drawer."

"Were you broken into?"

"No. One day I just noticed that it was gone. It could have been missing for ages, and I never noticed. I mentioned it to Joe over there, and he told me about his bank account."

No break-in, and no one knew. "Have you had anyone in your home, a stranger or a friend who could have stolen it?"

"I can't remember, love, but I don't think so, not strangers. My sister comes round, but she wouldn't take it. The man comes to read the lecky meter, but he stays in the hallway."

"Okay. If you do remember anything, just ring me."

Grace went to have a word with Joe. He'd not lost any jewellery but his bank account had been accessed without his consent.

"I check it all the time," he told her. "We'd been doing about online banking with Marshy. He's a good lad, set it all up for me."

"Did he know your log-in details? You know, password and the like?" Grace asked.

"Well, yes, love. I'm all fingers and thumbs. I couldn't get it right at the start. When the money went missing, I went into my branch and they changed everything for me."

"And you've not told anyone your log-in details since?"

"No. They said not to."

Grace went over to Joel. "Anything?"

"Max Marsh has gone through online banking with them. He's also helped one or two set up their computers at home. That means he had the opportunity to look around."

"I wonder if he went to Doreen's? He's been busy, has Marshy, don't you think? Have a word and I'll speak to the others."

Most of the pieces were identified and logged. They belonged to half a dozen of the group. Grace gathered the owners together. "Are any of you aware of a break-in at your homes?"

There was a unanimous shaking of heads.

"In that case, you either knew them, or they knew where to get hold of a key."

A man called Ernest Knowles spoke up. "Whoever it was must have been bloody quick. My cigarette case disappeared after I'd been to the bookies. I know because I'd had it out, showing a mate that morning. When I got back, it was gone."

"And your mate couldn't have taken it?"

"No. He left, and I put it back in the drawer. When I got back, everything was normal, exactly like I'd left it. Except for my cigarette case, that is."

"Did Marshy come to your house, help you set your computer up?" Grace asked.

"He did, love," Ernest Knowles replied. "He came once or twice until things were working right."

"He's been to most of our homes," Doreen told her. "He's keen to help and comes in his spare time."

"Keen to help, eh? I bet he is," Grace whispered to Joel.

"What's going on?" Dee came into the room and immediately clocked the display of jewellery.

"Theft," Grace told her. "Someone has been targeting the group."

The girl said nothing, but her hand flew unconsciously to her neck. She touched a round pendant, studded with red stones.

Grace nodded at it. "Nice. Where did you get it?"

"It's mine. Max gave it to me."

Grace looked round, but Marsh had made himself scarce. She made a mental note. "We will want to speak to you further, Dee," Grace warned her. "Both you and Max, so don't disappear."

# Chapter 14

Ava Whitton checked the two ID badges carefully before reluctantly admitting Greco and Grace into her home. "I have taken an hour off work, so this will have to be quick."

Greco felt his pulse quicken. The woman was as flawless as before. Her hair was wound into a neat plait at the back of her head. The expensive clothes she was wearing suited her tall, willowy frame perfectly. He had to get a grip. This woman was involved in their investigation up to her neck.

They followed her down the hallway and into the sitting room. "When we saw you the other day, you were adamant that you had not had a break-in," Greco began. "We have evidence that suggests that isn't true, Ms Whitton."

"What evidence?" she snapped back. "Do you imagine I wouldn't know if I'd been robbed? Do you think I'm stupid, Detective?"

"No, I think you are hiding something. I think there are things about your life that you do not want us to find out about."

"Utter rubbish! I don't like your tone. You have some nerve, coming to my home and spouting this fantasy."

Was she genuinely annoyed or trying to bluff her way out of it? Greco couldn't tell.

Grace held out the plastic bag containing the locket. "Does this belong to you?"

She stared at the object, looking stunned. "Where did you get that?"

"It was among the items stolen from this house," Grace replied calmly.

Ava Whitton looked at Greco with her dark eyes. Gone was the outraged bluster of before. Now she was genuinely afraid — and silently imploring him for help. She spoke in a barely audible whisper. "I cannot tell you anything. Because I do not know."

"But you were robbed?" Grace persisted.

Ava flopped down onto a chair, suddenly deflated, as if she'd given up. "Yes. I came home from work a few days ago and found the lock on a back window had been forced. There wasn't much mess, a broken vase that's all. But some money I had been saving and most of my jewellery had gone."

"Why didn't you report it?" Greco asked her kindly.

"I don't know. I should have done, but your colleagues came here that very day talking about there being drugs in my fridge. I was afraid. I thought I was being framed for a much more serious crime. Apart from which, there were only a few valuable pieces. My ring, the locket and a ruby pendant my grandmother gave me, and a valuable watch that belonged to my mother."

Grace thought of the pendant Dee had been wearing. The one Max had allegedly given her. "Do you have any photos of the jewellery?"

"Yes, for insurance purposes. I'll get them for you."

"You said they stole a ring. Do you recognise these?" Greco passed her their photograph. The rings themselves were still undergoing tests with Julian. "The maker's mark is the same on both."

Ava stared at the image for several seconds, her eyes wide and fearful. She handed Grace her own photos. "As you see, one of the rings is mine," she admitted, pointing to one of them. She looked at the detectives. "The other ring. Where did you get it?"

Greco could tell from the tremor in her voice that she was dreading his answer. "Why? Do you know who it belongs to?"

She was shaking. His reply was going to hurt.

"It was found on the body of a man," he said.

Ava buried her face in her hands and wept. "Tomasz! I knew something was wrong. I felt it inside me." She looked up at the detectives.

"Who was Tomasz?" Greco asked.

"My younger brother," she replied. "The rings were given to us by our parents. They were identical. Where exactly was he found?"

"Not too far from here. Roughly ten miles away."

"In that case, Tomasz was trying to get to me. He knew where I lived. He must have been in trouble. How long ago?"

"We don't know, not yet. It might help to know when you last saw or heard from him."

"We spoke on the phone ten months ago. Since then — nothing. He told me he was going away for a while."

"He was running from someone?" Grace asked.

"I don't know. Even if I'd asked he wouldn't have told me. I worried about Tomasz. He didn't always stay on the right side of the law. I was concerned that he was mixing with some dangerous people."

"Do you know who these people were?"

She shook her head. "He would never discuss it. But once or twice he asked me for money. How did he die? You have to tell me. Was he murdered?"

Greco decided not to tell her any details. Not yet. "Let us simply say that he didn't die of natural causes. His body was found in a Cheshire field," he said gently.

"A field? What was he doing there?"

"It was the site of a music festival last summer. Did your brother attend that sort of thing?" Grace asked.

Ava shook her head.

"The lads who broke into your house were also murdered," Greco told her. "There is a link between their murder and that of your brother."

"What are you saying? What link?"

Greco could hardly tell her it was the horrific way they'd met their end. "The rings. Possibly more. Because of that I want to send a forensic team in to search your house. They are looking for anything that will help find their killer. It will also help us find out who killed your brother. Because of the jewellery, we now know for sure that the lads were here in your home. They will have left forensic traces that could help us."

"Okay," she said at once. "Do whatever you have to."

"Before we leave you in peace, what was your brother's full name, Ms Whitton?" Greco asked.

"Tomasz Bilinski."

"You're Polish?" Grace asked.

Ava nodded.

"Was your brother allergic to anything?" Greco asked.

"Yes, peanuts. The merest trace could make him terribly ill."

"You use a different surname. Are you married?" asked Greco.

"No. I legally changed my name. I found having an English name more convenient for work. I have lived here for most of my life. I have very little accent left, so why not?" She shrugged.

* * *

Once the detectives had left, Ava broke down completely. Tomasz was dead. She didn't want to believe it, but she doubted the police had made a mistake. Weeping was not going to solve her problems. Ava knew that she was taking a risk allowing the forensic people into her home. She had been extra careful when she'd moved the heroin, but was that enough? Then there were the thieves. How careless had they been? Ava had scrubbed everywhere, but as she looked around her home, she doubted that even she had gotten rid of every trace. If the smallest trace of heroin was found here, the police would arrest her. It would not take them long to piece things together. The fact that she worked for a transport firm that travelled mostly to Eastern Europe would put her firmly in the frame.

It didn't take Ava long to decide that she wanted two things. To disappear completely, so as not to have to suffer the flak once the police learned of her true part in this affair. And she had no doubt that they would. The second thing — to get even with her brother's killer. To make Barton pay. Her problem now was to work out how to do it.

# Chapter 15

Day 5

The first task for the following day was to speak to Max Marsh and Dee. Greco sent uniformed officers to bring them in separately. He didn't want to give the pair a last minute opportunity to work out a story. Max Marsh was first. He'd been fingerprinted and was sitting in an interview room facing Greco and Grace.

"Do you know why you are here?" Greco asked the young man.

Max responded with a shake of the head and a shrug.

"You are aware that I was at the centre yesterday afternoon, and spoke to members of your computing group?" Grace asked.

"So what?"

Marsh appeared not to be in the least worried by his arrest. He was giving short answers. He kept tipping his chair back, holding himself steady by gripping the edge of the desk. It was extremely irritating. "Because we think the missing stuff from the centre has something to do with you," Grace said.

"Me? You're wrong! Why would I? All it'd get me is a few bob. If I do a good job with that group, Graham will give me a reference so I can get into college. I've got plans. I'm not going to risk them."

"I disagree, Max." Greco forced a smile. "From my point of view, it looks like it has a lot to do with you. You appear to have everything sewn up. The group you interact with trust you absolutely, so much so that they have taken your advice, allowed you into their homes to install equipment and software. They have accepted your friends as being trustworthy too."

"No one forced them. We were just being helpful. Nothing wrong in that."

"You've been to all the homes where things have been stolen," Grace told him.

"Craig and Vinny have been to folk's homes too. Some of the group needed help with other stuff, decorating and the like. One old dear needed some furniture moving. They did that for her. We're Clovelly's angels, remember?" He smiled. "And think about it, copper. You got none of that stolen stuff from me. You can search my place till the cows come home, and you'll still find nowt."

That was true. They didn't have solid evidence that Marsh was involved, but Greco reckoned he had to be. At the very least, he'd been the eyes and ears of their operation, and he'd got them all inside the houses. "Did Craig and Vinny give you anything to keep for them?"

"Like what? More cheap jewellery?" Marsh scoffed.

"No, like drugs. Heroin for example."

"No! Absolutely not. I have nothing to do with that stuff."

"Do you know a woman called Ava Whitton?" Greco asked him.

"No. Should I?"

"Are you sure? You've never heard the name?"

"No. Told you. Whatever she says, she's lying. Who is she anyway? Some relative of one of the group?"

"No, Max, she's the woman your pals robbed the other day. Some of the jewellery we found belonged to her." Greco paused, giving Marsh time to ponder this.

"That means Craig and Vinny must have taken stuff off the seniors too. Stands to reason," Marsh said at last.

"Do you recognise this?" Grace placed a photo of Ava's ruby pendant on the table.

"No. Never seen it before."

"I saw this yesterday. Your friend Dee was wearing it."

Greco watched Max Marsh fidget on the chair. Now the nerves were showing. "She told my colleague here that you gave it to her."

"Well, I didn't. Dee is lying as usual. Speak to her. Drag her in here. Make her tell you the truth."

"Don't worry, Max, we'll be doing just that very shortly," Greco said. "But it will go better for you if you tell us the truth."

Max Marsh didn't look happy with that at all. "She'll lie," he insisted. "You mustn't be taken in. She's very good at it. I'm not taking the blame for her or anyone else. I didn't steal that stuff."

"Tell us about Joe Davies' online banking account," Grace said. "He had money stolen from it. How do you think that happened?"

"I think the old gentleman made a mistake."

"I think you knew his details and helped yourself," Greco said.

"Prove it. It's just your word against mine."

"It still remains that the jewellery was stolen. I think you were as involved as Craig and Vinny. Do you have any theories to offer, Max?" Greco looked hard at him.

"Like I said before, nowt to do with me. Could have been anyone, there's a lot of thieving about."

Greco was getting angry. Until forensics gave them something, Max Marsh was right. They had nothing on him. He would swear that Dee was lying and no doubt she would do the same, and blame him. Greco could see where this was going — stalemate. Marsh's word against Dee's. "Okay, you can go," he told him reluctantly. "But we will speak to you again."

As soon as Marsh left, Grace said, "He has to be involved."

"Up to the teeth. But we need evidence before we can charge him," Greco replied.

Grace looked at him. "What now?"

"We get that young woman Dee in here, and see what she has to say for herself." He checked his watch. "We'll give it a little longer. Let her sweat a bit."

Greco and Grace went back to the incident room. Finding who was behind the pilfering at the centre was one thing, but what they really needed was information on the heroin.

Greco was staring at the board. "Drug smuggling is at the bottom of this, and that takes some organising. There have to be more people involved than just Ava Whitton. She is a cog in a much larger wheel."

"She was taking a risk too," Speedy added. "Keeping all that stuff in her fridge. Why would she do that?"

"I don't know, but you're right. Visit Greysons later. Speak to folk, see what you can find out. Ava Whitton plays a key role in bringing the stuff into the country. That firm she works for is the perfect cover." Greco tapped the firm's name. "Right industry, and she's the transport manager."

"She doesn't seem the type, sir. How would she manage an operation like that?" Speedy asked. "There's customs for example. Lorries like Greysons' are searched. Particularly these days, with people-trafficking so rife. There are dogs specially trained to sniff out drugs. Can't be done on the scale you reckon she's shipping them in."

"Obviously it can," Greco said. "Don't be duped by a pretty face. She's a clever woman. If there is a way to get around the searches, she will have found it."

"And the reason she didn't report the robbery at her house was because she was involved," Grace offered.

Grace had a point. "Let's get the next interview over with and then we'll talk about this some more. Meanwhile, I want to know a great deal more about Greyson Logistics."

"I'm on it, guv," Speedy said.

* * *

"What is your full name?" Grace asked the young woman.

"Deidre Sampson, but I prefer Dee. I mean, who calls their kid Deidre in this day and age?"

Grace smiled. "You're still wearing that nice pendant. You told me that Max gave it to you. When was that?"

"A few days ago. Why? What's your interest in an old bit of jewellery?"

Grace didn't reply, just watched her reaction. Dee looked wary. Her black-rimmed eyes darted nervously from one detective to the other.

Grace smiled again. "Are you sure it was Max who gave it to you? It was stolen, along with several other pieces. So, come on, where did you really get it from?"

"I'm not lying. Marshy really did give it to me," Dee insisted.

"Why would he do that? Was it a present or payment for something?"

"He just wanted me to have it." She shrugged. "It's no big deal."

Grace wasn't smiling now. "I'm afraid it is, Dee. You see it's part of the haul that Craig and Vinny took before they ended up dead. Hence our interest."

Now the girl looked shocked. "I had nothing to do with that. You'll have to speak to Marshy, ask him about it." Her hands went to her neck and she undid the clasp. "Here, take it. I swear the bloody thing is cursed! I've had nothing but aggro since he gave it to me!"

"Our problem is that he denies knowing anything about the pendant. So that leaves you in the frame, Dee."

The girl's eyes widened. "He knows very well. He gave it to me and I gave him forty quid to pay a bill. Ask him. Tell him what I've just told you. Don't let him wriggle out of it. He came to me because he's known by all the local pawnshops. He regularly tries to sell stolen gear. He's been done for it in the past. I've done nothing. How could I? I don't know anything about what that lot get up to. Angels." She rolled her eyes. "Who are they kidding? A group of lowlife scum who'd rob their own mothers if the opportunity presented itself. I'm telling you, the thieving, it will be down to those lads with Marshy's help."

"Everything you've told us will go in your statement, Dee, and you will sign it," Greco told her.

Dee nodded. "No probs. I haven't done anything. You've got it wrong. Go and arrest Marshy. Like I said, he's dodgy at the best of times."

"Did he offer you any drugs?"

"No, just the pendant."

"Have you heard any talk about heroin at the centre?" Greco asked her. "Perhaps someone new with stuff to sell?"

"I'm not interested. Never take drugs. But as far as I know there is nothing new on that front."

# Chapter 16

"You look tired," Greco said.

"Thanks for that. You really know how to boost a girl's ego!" Grace replied.

Greco hadn't meant the comment to be taken as an insult. He was genuinely concerned about Grace. She was pale and didn't have her usual energy. "Why not call it a day? Take yourself off home."

"It's only lunchtime. What will the others say?"

"I'll sort it. Don't worry. Actually, I was thinking of telling them, after I've told McCabe of course."

"He won't like it. Have you thought about the repercussions?"

"He will have to know at some time."

Grace looked at him. "Don't you want to leave the team to me?"

"Not this time. I'm quite capable, you know. Go and put your feet up while Holly is still at school."

They were walking back to the incident room, along the corridor. "What d'you think?" she asked. "Max Marsh or Dee? Which one is telling the truth?"

"I think they are both lying to save their own skins. Perhaps Dee not so much. They are frightened of something, and it's more than just going down for theft or receiving," Greco said.

Grace frowned. "You think they know something about the drugs?"

"Yes, I do. This afternoon I'll arrange for forensics to go over Ava Whitton's house. We know Vinny had traces of heroin under his fingernail. If they opened one of those packets in that house there will be traces left behind," Greco said.

"Do you believe Dee on the drugs front?" she asked.

"We need more evidence first. But we are moving forward. We now know some of that jewellery was stolen from Ava Whitton, so Craig and Vinny were at her house. And thanks to Ava, we now have a name for 'Festival Fred.' I'm sure Julian will call that a result." He smiled faintly.

Grace winced and caught her breath.

"You okay?" Greco asked.

She touched her stomach. "I've got a headache and I think there must have been something dodgy about that seafood salad I ate earlier."

Greco pulled a face. "Don't know how you can. Prawns and the like have never been my thing, especially for breakfast."

"I'm pregnant, Stephen. I fancy something, I eat it. I think I will go home. I'm dead on my feet."

"Do you want a lift?" he asked.

"No, I'll be fine. My car is in the car park."

"Take care. I'll ring you later."

\* \* \*

Greco updated the incident board and went to find Leah.

"I had a word with Roman. He doesn't like the Ashtree. Apparently it's frequented by some dodgy characters." She pulled a face. "Coming from Roman, that's some statement. And what pub is dodgier than the Grapes, I ask you?" Leah said.

"Did he know anything?"

She shook her head. "Nothing about the town being awash with drugs, if that's what you mean. There's no one new dealing either."

"Craig and Vinny must have put that haul somewhere. Those packets didn't just disappear into thin air. We've searched their homes — nothing." Greco sighed.

"They could have passed them on. And whoever they gave them to is sitting on the stash until things quieten down," Leah said.

"Ava Whitton is Polish by birth. She works at Greyson Logistics. I've got Speedy taking a closer look at the firm. But we need more. Find out who drives for them, and what routes they cover."

Greco was staring at the incident board again. What were they missing? Jewellery had gone missing from Ava's house and the community centre. That had to be down to Craig and Vinny with help from Max Marsh. Perhaps it was him who gave them the information as to who had what worth stealing. But was Marsh involved in the theft of the drugs too? He'd have another word with Clovelly, ask him to keep an eye out. Speedy and Leah were discussing Greysons. Joel had his eyes glued to his computer screen.

"I'm going out," Greco called to them.

"Want company?" Speedy asked.

"No. I'm going to the centre again. Another word with Clovelly. I won't be long."

* * *

"I'm looking for the boss," the man said.

DI Leah looked up from her desk and smiled at the stranger who had just spoken. He was about her age, mid-thirties, and he was flashing a badge. He didn't return her smile.

"DI Grant Chambers, drug squad."

"DI Leah Wells," she said. "DCI Greco is the boss, but he's not here, I'm afraid. He's out doing his job. Chasing villains," she said pointedly. "What can I do for you?"

"You lot can get your size tens out of our case for a start. My guvnor doesn't like amateurs bumbling into things that don't concern them."

Leah was taken aback. He had some cheek coming into their incident room and laying down the rules. Red with anger, she stood up and faced him. "I beg your pardon! You can't come in here and tell us what we can and can't do. And we are not 'bumbling' into anything, as you put it. We are investigating two murders. We speak to who we need to, and go where the case leads us, until a higher rank than you tells us to lay off."

"The heroin. Ava Whitton. Leave it alone." His tone was sharp, authoritative. He'd taken no notice of what she'd just said.

"That sounds like a threat, DI Chambers."

"It's a warning. We're close to winding up a case we've been working for eighteen months. We won't allow you lot to ruin it. So, I repeat, back off. Or that 'higher rank,' as you put it, will come down on you like a ton of bricks!"

"You need to drop the attitude. Why don't we try talking instead? Tell me what you know, and I'll do likewise. We could help each other."

"No. Keep out of our way. You are straying into very dangerous waters, DI Wells. The people involved are killers."

Leah looked him in the eye. "We are fully aware of that! We've got three bodies in the morgue. I can't describe that has been done to them. We know what we're doing, Inspector. We are not amateurs."

"A piece of advice for you. Take Whitton's name off that board and leave the woman alone." With that, he turned on his heel and left the room.

* * *

Dee was angry. Getting dragged down to the police station was not supposed to happen. Damn those lads and their stupid scams, and damn Marshy for saddling her with the pendant. As soon as she got out of the station, she rang her boyfriend. "I've got the police sniffing around. Those lads have ballsed things up big style. That idiot Marshy gave me stolen jewellery. I've been wearing the stuff and the police spotted it."

"Are you being watched?" Dom said.

"I don't think so."

"Did you tell them anything about me?"

"No, of course not. Anyway, there's nothing to tell. There isn't, is there, Dom?" Dee was worried. On the surface, Dom appeared okay — the epitome of a clean-living, law-abiding young man. But Dee knew that wasn't the truth. Dom came from a rough background. He knew people, people like Barton. He and Barton had something going, but she didn't know what.

"No, I've told you. Me, I'm whiter than white. What about Barton? Did his name come up?"

"No. I don't think the police know anything about him. I'm not telling Barton about the police, and don't you either. It'll make him edgy. He wants to meet later. I'm waiting for a text."

"Take care. Don't trust him, and watch your back. The man has a filthy temper."

Dee had no sooner finished talking to Dom when her mobile rang again. This time it was Barton.

"The house on Balfour Street, Gorton, in thirty minutes, and don't be late. It's the one with the 'to let' sign outside. I have a job for you."

Short and sweet. The upside of working for Barton was that he paid well. There was no time to go to the centre first and get a coffee, which she'd been planning to do. She'd have to get the bus. It wasn't far to the meet but it was raining hard. She was dressed in jeans and a hoodie, and would soon be soaked.

On her way to the bus stop, Dee thought about Dom, and his relationship with Barton. She'd have to be careful, and be sure not to let anything slip. Dom was okay with her up to a point, but he was crafty. His loyalty went to whoever paid him the most. Currently that was Barton. Dee wasn't daft. The police were looking for missing drugs. The theft had something to do with Vinny and Craig, and they'd ended up dead. How those two idiots had managed to outwit drug traffickers she didn't know. But they must have had inside information. It was rumoured that Barton was a major player in the drug dealing that went on in this area of the city. What concerned her was that Dom might be somehow mixed up in that too.

She was deep in thought when a car pulled up beside her. "Get in." It was a voice she recognised. "I'll give you a lift. Keep you long, did they?"

The ride was a godsend. Dee accepted the offer gladly, and relaxed back into the passenger seat. "Nice motor. Where did you get it from? It must have cost you a bit."

"Did a bit of business."

"You were parked up over there. I saw the car as I came around the corner. Were you waiting for me?"

"No, I'm on my way home. Stopped to take a call. What did the police ask you?"

Another one wanting to know what had gone on. Dee wasn't daft. He must have been waiting and watching if he knew where she'd been. "They are poking around into a bit of bother at the centre. You know, the stolen jewellery. Trouble is the bastard police have got it all wrong. I've done nowt, but they don't believe me. That idiot Marshy is at the bottom of this."

"Where are you off to?"

"I've got to meet someone in Gorton. A job that could bring in wages this week." She smiled.

"A meet? Anyone I know?"

Dee shook her head. "I doubt it. Owner of an old house on Balfour Street that's being done up to be let out. Makes a bloody fortune with his scams, the man does."

"You're talking about Barton."

"You amaze me sometimes. How do you know Barton?" She was genuinely surprised. Dom had told her that outside his own circle, Barton kept a low profile these days.

He ducked a direct reply. "You want to be careful, Dee. You're mixing with trouble there. At the first sign of interest from the police, Barton will drop you right in it."

"I can look after myself."

He was speeding down the dual carriageway. Suddenly he turned onto a back street Dee didn't recognise. He grinned. "Short cut."

"Slow down, idiot. You don't have to show off in front of me. You'll kill someone at this rate!"

The car screeched to a halt in the shadow of a disused warehouse. The houses on the other side of the road were empty and scheduled for demolition.

"Hey! This isn't Balfour Street."

"It's as near as you're going."

"Look, I don't know what this is all about, but I'm not interested." Dee presumed that it was some sort of come-on. She tried the door, pulled at the handle for all she was worth, but it was locked. He made a grab for her. "You're a bloody animal!" she screamed.

Seconds later, Dee felt something sharp pierce her upper arm. The effect of whatever he'd given her was almost immediate. Dee felt unreal, like she was floating. Then she fell sideways and knew no more.

# Chapter 17

Just as Greco pulled onto the spare ground in front of the community centre, his mobile rang. It was Emily Harper, Grace's mum.

Her voice was strained. "Grace is in hospital. She arrived home in a right state, in pain and throwing up. I took her to the maternity department, and they want to keep her in."

Greco didn't know what to say. He was afraid that if he said anything, Emily would spot the relief in his voice and jump to the wrong conclusion. She'd believe he was pleased that this whole sorry mess might be about to end, and the decision whether to continue the pregnancy taken out of their hands.

"I'll go and see her," he replied calmly.

"It might be nothing. Grace thinks I'm fussing, but she's not right and I want her looked at. I can't stay with her because I've got to see to Holly."

"Leave Grace to me," he told her gently. "I'll keep you posted."

As he was getting out of his car, Graham Clovelly pulled up beside him.

"Back again. Aren't the kids twitchy enough?" he said.

"Just want to clear a few things up. Can we speak in private?"

"I have to open up. You've had Marshy and Dee down at the station. Wasn't that enough?"

"I needed to speak to them both," Greco said. "But there is still a great deal about this case we don't know."

"We'll talk in the café."

Greco followed Graham into the building. Within minutes the place began to fill up with youngsters. Max Marsh was already in the adjoining room, setting out equipment.

"The thefts. Who do you think is responsible?" Greco asked Graham outright.

"I've no idea. What with that and the murders, I'm at my wits' end. I didn't even know it was going on. On the surface, it looks like it has to have been Craig and Vinny, possibly with help from Marshy. But he must have been coerced. He's a good lad. He has a past, but he's put all that behind him. Come next September, he wants to do an IT course at the college. Get properly qualified, and find a job that pays well. He's on track too. He's been going to night classes to get the GCSEs he should have done at school. He isn't going to risk all that work for a bit of ready cash."

"Who else did Craig and Vinny trust in the group? Who would be likely to join them?"

"Any one of them. All the youngsters have had difficult backgrounds. If Craig or Vinny was offering a quick way of getting hold of some money, they would be sorely tempted. For all I know, the whole lot could have taken the stuff between them."

"How do you reckon Dee got hold of a piece of jewellery stolen from the house in Handforth?"

That threw Graham for a moment. "Perhaps one of the lads gave it to her. They all like Dee. Did you ask her?"

"Yes, I did. She said that Marsh gave it to her. Sold it to her, in effect."

Graham shook his head. "He didn't steal it. I'd stake my life on it. Of all the youngsters who come here, he's the soundest."

"Okay. The others who come here. What about them?"

"They don't give me any trouble. They come here mostly to practise on the pool table. They help out. They have a laugh, sit about and socialise. Occasionally they interact with the groups.

"Does Callum Riley come here? Is he one of your angels?"

"He comes here sometimes and helps out with the activities. He is one of the angels. He does a lot of work with the food bank. He's in the pool team too. Not as good a player as his brother. I won't be able to use him for a while — what's happened will have thrown him. They weren't particularly close, him and Craig, but they were twins."

"In what way, not close?" Greco asked. He'd heard this before, and it sparked his curiosity. "Did they fight?"

"Occasionally. I know Callum didn't always approve of Craig's behaviour. Craig had a short fuse. Callum was always trying to straighten him out. When common sense and words didn't work, they would scrap. I had to split them up frequently. It's possible that Callum knew the lads were up to something. During the few days before him and Vinny died, Craig and his brother weren't speaking at all. Made for a right atmosphere in here."

Greco made a mental note to speak to Callum. He knew the lad would still be grieving, but Greco needed information quickly. High on the list was what Craig had been planning in the last days of his life. "If you think of anything else, if you find out anything I should know about, contact me at once."

Greco left him to it.

* * *

A uniformed officer handed Leah Wells a sheet of paper. "You'll find this interesting. Came in about an hour ago. I recognised the name from your investigation — Ava Whitton. Apparently, she's had her purse stolen from a café in town. She told the officer who attended that someone was sitting at her table with her. She turned her back for a moment, and then her purse was gone. There is plenty of CCTV. The café is slap bang in the middle of Market Street. She's currently taking a look."

The officer was right, it was of interest. Leah could only guess at what it meant. "If she does pick him out, get the image to us pronto. Who knows, we might recognise him ourselves."

Joel Hough had overheard the conversation. "I rang Greysons," he said. "Made an appointment to go and have a chat. I asked to speak to Ava Whitton and they said she wasn't expected in. Ill, the receptionist told me. Obviously that's wrong, if she's drinking coffee in town."

"Go and take a look at that café before you go to Greysons," Leah said. "She may have simply fancied a day shopping, but then again . . . Ask the staff. See if they remember her."

Leah's mobile rang while she was updating the incident board. It was Roman.

"A couple of youngsters from the Lansdowne have been ferried to hospital in Oldston within the last hour. Took an overdose. Not on purpose. The stuff hadn't been cut properly. Too strong. Looks like we've got an amateur on the loose."

"Any names?"

"No, but the kids hang around the community centre."

Leah rang Greco but got no response. She decided to go to the hospital herself, and see if the two kids were up to talking.

They were an important lead. At the very least they'd know who had sold them the stuff. That was if Leah could get them to talk. There were still too many questions. Nothing they had so far fitted together correctly. Leah wanted to make headway on the case. She was ambitious. The move to Greco's team at serious crime was a step in the right direction, but it wasn't where she saw herself long term. She had her sights set on DCI, and a job with a team in the capital. It would mean another move, but that didn't bother her. Leah Wells was free and single. She was born in the Manchester area, but had no close family, and was more than happy to work wherever the job took her.

The two patients were in separate cubicles. One was still receiving treatment, but the other, a teenage girl, had regained consciousness. She was groggy, though. Her mother was sitting with her.

"I'm DI Wells from the serious crime squad. Do you mind if I have a word with her?"

"You won't get much. She's still out of it. Talking rubbish and being sick mostly," her mother said.

Leah nodded. Understandable. "I'll stick around for a bit, if you don't mind. Has she said anything about what she took, or where she got it?"

The girl's mother shook her head. "She was hanging around the estate after school. You can get your hands on anything there if you know who to ask. I blame that bloody boy she's been going around with."

"Which boy?" Leah asked.

"He goes to the community centre a lot. I don't know — one of them Riley boys, I think."

"Craig or Callum?"

"No idea. It might not even be them. Can't tell them apart these days. They all dress the bloody same."

"Have you given the officer your name and address?" Leah indicated the uniformed officer sat outside.

The woman nodded.

Leah decided to go and grab a coffee while she waited for the girl to come round. She spotted Greco on the stairs down to the café.

"Sir! You got the message?"

"What message?"

"About the drug overdoses. It looks as if our missing heroin has made its way onto the streets."

Greco shook his head. "I'm here on a different matter."

"I'm waiting to have a chat with the two girls, once they become coherent. But one thing — they hang out at the community centre. That clinches it. Someone there has to be involved."

"If whoever took the heroin has starting selling, they won't stop. Get Joel down there when he returns. Tell him to hang about, speak to Clovelly."

"Oh, and we've had a visit from the drug squad. A DI called Chambers. Right piece of work. Reckons we're stepping on toes. Ava Whitton has sneaked a day off work. She reckons a man stole her purse in a coffee shop in town. It's a weird one. I've sent Joel to check it out." Leah looked at him. She hadn't noticed before, but Greco was clutching flowers. Was he visiting someone? "You alright, sir? Someone close not well? It's not your daughter, is it?"

"No, Leah."

He clammed up in that way he had. It showed in his expression — tight-lipped and with furrowed brow. She'd get no more out of him. Leah watched him walk a little further, then buzz to enter the maternity department. Now Leah was really curious. She wondered who he knew who was pregnant or had just given birth.

* * *

Speedy decided to visit Greysons Logistics himself, leaving Joel to visit the café in Manchester. He pulled up in the yard and looked around. The firm had a nice spot on the Quays with a view of the waterfront from the two-storey office block. Business must be good. Properties here weren't cheap. A dozen or more lorries were parked up in a row outside. Speedy went into reception and asked for Martin Greyson. The young woman at the desk told him Greyson was out, and unlikely to be back today.

With a smile, Speedy showed her his ID. "I'm police. I'm speaking to all the local haulage firms who travel to Eastern Europe. Mind if I wander around, talk to some of the drivers?"

"They have their own café and staff room across the yard. One or two of them are in. Speak to whoever you like," she said.

So far, so good. Speedy made his way over to the café. The counter was manned by a young man of around twenty, who nodded. "Only sandwiches and drinks now."

"It's okay, I'm not here to eat."

A stocky bloke sitting at a corner table looked up. He was the only customer.

Speedy smiled at him. "Police. I've spoken to the office, and they say it's okay to ask you a few questions."

"Better make it quick, I'm about to get some rest. We hit the road tomorrow."

"Where are you going?"

"Warsaw."

"Your cargo?"

The man reached for a clipboard on the table and handed Speedy the manifest. "Fill your boots, mate."

"According to the paperwork, you are carrying stationery. Is that it?"

"This trip, yeah, but we carry a range of stuff. We have customers in a variety of industries, and we go all over the place."

"Anything ever go wrong on these trips?"

"You name it, it happens. Blowouts, engine failure, even robbery at gunpoint. We were threatened by terrorists not so long ago."

Speedy frowned. "Didn't realise it was such a tricky job. If something does go wrong, say, with the truck for example, what do you do?"

"Greyson has an arrangement with a number of garages along the routes we travel. They usually sort us out. Just as well. Despite being fairly new, some of the vehicles are prone to problems."

"Many people work the trucks?"

"A dozen or more. He does a brisk trade, does Greyson. Knows his stuff."

"Do you ever have any bother at customs?" asked Speedy.

"Not really. Mind you, last week they paid a visit here. Out of the blue. No warning. We had the buggers nosing around for days."

"Do you know why?"

"No idea, mate. Probably just routine. You'll have to speak to Greyson or Ms Whitton for that."

Speedy made a note to do that very thing.

"Can I help?"

Speedy turned around. Standing in the doorway was a smartly dressed young man in a dark suit.

"Dominic Hill. I work for Ms Whitton," the man said.

"In that case, perhaps you know why Customs and Excise were here last week?"

"A routine visit, they said. Checked a lot of paperwork. Went through the cargo on a couple of lorries. Basically, they made everyone nervous and got in the way." He smiled. "But they have a job to do."

"Did you know they were coming?"

"No. It was a spot check. We had no choice but to give them access to anything and everything."

"Did they find anything?"

"Like what?" Dominic Hill asked. "The stuff we transport is all very innocent, I promise you."

"Okay, thanks for your input," Speedy said.

# Chapter 18

Superintendent McCabe collared Greco on his return to the station. "You've been stepping on toes, Stephen. Not your usual style."

After his conversation with Leah, Greco knew what McCabe was on about — the drug squad visit. "Can't be helped, sir. We need to know a lot more about Ava Whitton. Sorting this case depends on it. Right now, I'd like to know what is behind this stolen purse — if that's what did happen. We need a lot more information about Greysons too. That firm she works for is suspect. Their lorries are going through the port of Dover to Calais and back constantly. They have been searched, the business premises have been searched, but nothing has been found. Our colleagues in the drug squad need to stop harassing us, or share what they've got."

"I don't know a lot more than you do. But your investigation has got the drug squad twitchy. Whether it's Ava Whitton they're after or the folk she works with, we'll have to see. She is involved with some ruthless people, Stephen."

"The problem is, sir, we don't know the first thing about these 'ruthless' people. However, she has agreed to a forensic search of her house." Greco checked his watch. "In fact, it should be going ahead as we speak."

"That won't please Chambers. His parting shot to DI Wells was to forget her."

"We both know that is not going to happen. Ava Whitton is in this up to her neck. The drug squad is not alone in knowing that she is key to the importation of heroin, and God knows what else."

"Tread carefully, Stephen. If you need any help with access to anything, let me know. I can't promise, but I'll do my best."

While they spoke, Greco spotted Speedy lurking further down the corridor.

He followed Greco into the incident room. "I think I know why Ava Whitton took the heroin to her house, sir. It had to be a spur of the moment thing. They had Customs and Excise round at Greysons. They descended without warning. If the stuff was in one of the lorries, she would have had to move it urgently."

"You think she simply took it home? Taking a bit of a risk, wasn't she? Plus, if she was just able to get her hands on it at the drop of a hat, why was it so difficult for customs at Dover to find?" Greco tapped a pencil on the desktop, thinking. "If the stuff was still in one of the lorries at Greysons, how is it moved on from there?"

"I take your point, sir," Speedy said. "But what is even more interesting is that Riley and Holt chose that very day to carry out the robbery. Not by chance, I think. Someone at Greysons has to have known those lads, and told them. But who?"

"Ring and get a list of employees," Greco told him. "They could have employed anyone. They were about to take on Craig Riley, remember."

"Do we know in what capacity?"

"Well, he couldn't drive a lorry. Too young. While you're at it, perhaps you'd like to find out."

"What's happened to Grace?" Speedy asked.

"She's gone home, not feeling very well," Greco replied. He decided not to say anything just yet. He'd see how the next day or so went. If Grace lost the baby, there would be no need to say anything at all. If not, McCabe first and then the team.

Joel returned from his visit into Manchester. "Whether the man stole her purse or not, Ava Whitton knows who he is," he announced to the team. "According to the waiter, they were chatting for a while. He was waiting and when she arrived, she went and sat with him."

"What is she up to?" asked Greco. "We need to speak to her again."

Joel went to his desk and checked his PC. "The photo of the man she met is through, sir."

Greco went over to take a look. "Do we know him?"

"I do," Speedy said, looking over Joel's shoulder. "That's Alex Barton, a local businessman. Or so he describes himself. He's a property developer. Buys cheap at auction, does them up and then lets them out. Not that he spends much money. It's all gloss. His properties are some of the shoddiest in the area, but he's still got tenants all over Greater Manchester. Most of them unhappy. A bit of a wide boy when it comes to tenancy agreements is Barton. He keeps them short, a matter of months. And he's quick to turf folk out if he can get a higher rent."

"Why would Ava Whitton meet him? She doesn't rent that house in Handforth, does she?"

Speedy laughed. "Rent off him? You're joking. Your seedy backstreet terrace is more his line."

"Nevertheless, there has to be some connection," Greco said. "We need to find it. Ava Whitton is key to solving this, and it is possible that Barton has some part in it too." He looked at Joel. "Get some background on the man. Let's see what he's been up to recently. Check if he has any connection with Greysons."

"I'm going to get off," Speedy said.

Greco nodded. It was getting late. He should go home and tell Pat about Grace. After that, another visit to the hospital.

* * *

Pat Greco was upset at the news. "You should have rung me straight away, Stephen. I would have gone and seen her."

Greco pulled a face. "You have enough to do. Besides, you've got Matilda to pick up from school."

"We'll have something to eat, then you go. If Grace is still in tomorrow, I'll visit her then. But make sure she knows that you didn't tell me. She'll think no one cares!"

"Grace will more than likely be home tomorrow. A bit of tummy-ache, that's all it is."

"You are such a fool at times, Stephen. You really have no idea, have you? Grace is thrilled about this baby. If anything happens, if she should lose it, she will be devastated."

"Would it really be so bad?"

"I don't know how you can stand there and say that, Stephen Greco! That baby is yours too. Get your head straight, for goodness sake. If this is just a blip, then the infant will be a reality within a few months. Start taking responsibility."

That was him told! He was about to tell Pat how difficult this was going to make things at work when the phone rang. It was Joel Hough.

"Sorry, sir, I wouldn't have rung if I didn't have to. We have a body. Found in a ginnel running along the back of Balfour Street, Gorton. According to Dr Bowers, she's not been dead long." There was a pause. "Dr Bowers says it looks a lot like the killing of the two lads, sir."

"Do we have an ID?"

117

"I'm afraid it's Dee Sampson."

# Chapter 19

Dee Sampson had been hit so hard that the back of her skull was caved in. She was lying face up on the flagstones in a passageway that ran behind Balfour Street. It had been raining, and her clothing was wet and bedraggled. Her distinctive white, spiked-up hair was bloody and flattened against her head.

"It looks like a single blow. Delivered with enough force to kill her," Dr Bowers confirmed. "As for the rest of it — similar to the lads. Fingers cut off, an attempt made to ram them down her throat. An unsuccessful go at setting her alight, failed due to all the rain. Despite using an accelerant, the downpour we've had this afternoon must have dowsed the flames. Lucky. It gives us something to work with. She still has all her clothing intact too."

"Perhaps he was disturbed," Joel Hough said.

Greco agreed. "It does look like the killer didn't have a lot of time." He turned to the two uniformed officers who were standing nearby. "Knock on a few doors. There are several windows overlooking the area. Someone might have seen something. Find out who owns these properties too."

"This isn't where she was killed, Stephen," said Bob Bowers. "There isn't a lot of blood, but there is enough to leave drag marks from the curb to here."

"So why would our killer want to leave her in this particular spot?" Greco looked around him. It was another of those depressing, grey backstreets. All terraced houses with no gardens, and everyone fighting for a parking space. "Go with the uniforms," he told Joel. "Make sure the three of you do a thorough job of speaking to the folk who live around here. Strange cars, anyone suspicious in the area, you know the stuff."

"I will have more for you once the PM is done," said Bob Bowers. "Sometime tomorrow. I'll let you know ASAP, Stephen."

About to join the others, Joel turned back to Greco. "Why her, d'you reckon, sir?"

"She knew something, and spoke to the wrong person. Dee would have been a lot better off trusting us. She was only in the station this morning. Both her and Marsh were interviewed about the jewellery theft. We need to speak to him. I want a detailed breakdown of his whereabouts today."

"I'll get on it when I get back, sir."

Greco looked at the young DC. "You speak to the residents here. I'll find Marsh. The centre is still open. That's our best bet."

Greco rang the station and made a request for the CCTV from outside their building and the immediate area to be made available. He wanted to map Dee's movements from when she left them earlier. He would go to the centre first, then call at the Riley house and arrange a meeting with Callum.

The community centre was busy. Inside, a couple of groups were still busy, and a number of youngsters were standing around chatting outside.

Graham Clovelly sat at a table in the café, elbow deep in paperwork. "Schedule for the coming months. I've got a host of new classes to factor in. We're popular. Folk are asking for different activities all the time."

Greco sat down beside him. He got straight to the point. "Max Marsh. Is he in?"

"Yes, he's in his room with a group. Do you want him?"

"How long has he been here?"

"He was proper put out by you lot today. Not been himself since. He came back from the station in a right state. He believes that you're going to pin the lot on him, and he's scared. Like me, he's not moved out of the building all day. Kept his head down, and kept busy."

"Not even to get some lunch, or nip home?" Greco asked.

"No, at lunchtime he helped me with a delivery, then we ate in here."

"Did Dee come back here?" Greco asked.

"She hasn't been here at all today, which is odd for her. Why the interest? What's happened?"

This was going to upset him. Dee was a big part of what went on here. "Dee has been murdered, Graham," Greco told him. "We found her about an hour ago."

Graham looked at Greco, his eyes moist. "And you thought Marshy was responsible." He shook his head. "I've told you. You've got the lad all wrong. Besides, he could never kill anyone. He's fond of Dee. He enjoys what he does here. The centre is a stepping stone. He's got plans and he isn't about to balls it up."

"I will need a word with Marsh."

Graham got up and went to fetch him.

Superficially it looked as if Marsh was their man. Probably an argument with Dee about what was said during the interviews that got out of hand. But if he had a cast-iron alibi, then who?

"I left the nick and came straight here," Marsh said without being asked. Graham had obviously told him what had happened. "I didn't wait for Dee. She'd lied about that bloody necklace thing and I was angry with her." He hung his head. "Wish I'd waited now. Perhaps she'd still be alive if I'd brought her back with me."

"Do you know who Dee's friends were, apart from the ones here?"

Marsh shook his head. "Not really. She mixed with some weird types. Just lately she'd taken up with some bloke. He wasn't her type at all. Wore a suit to work for a start."

"Do you know his name?"

"Dee said nowt about him. I did ask. It's no secret that I liked her. But she always clammed up."

"Thank you." Greco sighed. "I'll send someone round to take your statement."

On his way back to the station, Greco called in at the Riley house. Mrs Riley answered the door. He could see from her face that she'd been weeping.

"Why won't you give him back?" was the first thing she said. "I want to bury him. He's my son. It isn't decent to keep his family waiting like this."

"It won't be long now," Greco assured her. "Is Callum in?"

She left him standing at the door while she went off to get him. Greco had never seen Craig in the flesh, but he had seen plenty of photos. His mouth fell open. The young man behind her was the spitting image of his brother.

"Are you up to talking to me yet?" Greco began. "I want to know a lot more about Craig's life. Where he went, who he saw. Particularly in the few days before he was killed. Vinny and him were planning the robbery in Handforth. Did he let anything slip?"

"He didn't." Greco saw the hate in the lad's eyes. It was still too early. He would have to wait. Problem was,

Greco wanted to wrap this up before more of the stuff hit the street.

Callum leaned forward. "Look, copper. I don't want my mother upset any more than she is already. She isn't up to this yet. She might not want to hear it but Craig was a moron, end of. He didn't trust me, so he didn't tell me ' owt, and I didn't ask. With our Craig it was best to stay well out of it. He spent his time with Vinny, not us. The sooner we get him laid to rest, the better for her in there."

So much for being the gentle one. Callum could obviously give as good as he got.

* * *

Greco decided to go to the hospital next. It was nearly seven in the evening, visiting time.

He genuinely didn't know how he felt about what had happened to Grace. Earlier today he'd believed that if she lost the baby, it would set things right again. But of course, it wouldn't. Things were not that simple. He was still wrestling with his emotions, and how he felt about Grace. With Suzy it had been simple. He'd been captivated from the first moment he set eyes on her. With Grace, she had made all the running. He knew he was being unfair. There was *something* between them. Had to be, they had a baby on the way. But if that was the case, why had he been so taken with Ava Whitton when he'd first set eyes on her? If he really loved Grace, he shouldn't have reacted like that. Greco realised that he still had a lot of thinking to do before he made any decision.

A nurse let him into the room. Grace was alone, dressed and sitting on the bed, reading a magazine. She smiled.

"Have you come to take me home? They said I could go before teatime. Mum couldn't pick me up, she's looking after Holly."

"You're alright? The baby? Is it . . . ?"

"Yes, we're both fine."

There was something in her eyes. A question. Greco knew he should reassure her, take control like Pat wanted, but he couldn't.

"Apparently, it was down to that bloody salad. If I get the urge to eat anything like that again, stop me."

He saw the look. Grace was analysing his body language. He should at least take her in his arms. Tell her he was pleased, and that he'd look after things from now on. But neither the actions nor the words would come.

"Try and crack a smile, Stephen. It's good news. The babe is still on track."

"Sorry. I was worried that you might have . . ."

"What — lost it? No such luck." There was anger and disappointment in her voice. "You would have preferred that, wouldn't you? Problem gone, no decision taken by you or me. The hand of fate and all that."

He could not answer that.

"You are a piece of work! You make me so mad, Greco. We. Are. Having. This. Baby. Get used to it. I will be back at work tomorrow, and it's my intention to tell folk. This can't stay a secret any longer. Apart from which, I have maternity leave to sort."

"Let me tell the team, and McCabe first."

She had that doubtful look on her face again. "If they don't know by lunch, you're toast. Got it?"

What was the use? She was right.

# Chapter 20

Day 6

Vasili Pakulski packed a small suitcase with what he thought he might need for the trip. He was out of his depth. He'd never had a job like this before. He was more used to short hauls, no more than fifty miles a trip. He liked to get home at night. Take care of his family. But in order to keep his landlord, Barton, sweet, he had no choice but to take what had been put on the table. He had been warned by friends who also rented from Barton, and knew better than him what the man was capable of. Barton was not a man to cross. You did as you were told. Vasili was stuck with things as they were. It was the job with Greysons, whether he liked it or not.

They set off from the lorry park at Salford Quays at five in the morning. George Potts, the driver, made no attempt to talk to him. Vasili didn't know if it was because of his own poor English, or if the man was simply rude. Consequently, all the way to Dover they mostly had only the radio for company. When they reached the port, Vasili rang his wife, Nadia. He tried to keep it upbeat.

"The job is easy. We are still travelling," he told her in Polish. "All I have to do is sit and watch the countryside go by."

"You will be gone for days," she protested. "I don't like it. Your old job was fine, and it paid well enough."

She was upset, and rightly so. "You know the score, Nadia. I work for Mr Barton, or we lose the house. Until I can find something better, we have no choice."

George Potts was beckoning him. He'd climbed back into the cab and started the engine. Vasili knew Potts would not wait. Customs sorted, he was ready to drive onto the ferry.

"I have to go. I'll phone you later."

"Once we're on board the ferry, stretch your legs, have some breakfast. But don't get lost," Potts warned him. "When we get the call to return to the vehicle, I won't come looking. We still have a long way to go." Potts nudged him. "There is a schedule to stick to. We'll stop for the night at a place I know, another hundred miles or so. It's nowt special. A café with cheap beds. If you can't afford it, then the cab's all yours." He grinned.

Barton or no Barton, Vasili knew then that he could not continue to earn his living this way. He would have to find alternative accommodation for his family.

\* \* \*

Bob Bowers had arranged Dee's post-mortem for ten that morning. Greco went to the station first to check if anything had come in overnight. Grace was at her desk.

"I thought you might take a couple of days off," Greco muttered.

"No, Stephen, you were hoping I would. That would get you out of telling the others, wouldn't it?" She looked up at him. "Well, I'm here, and we have a bargain. Lunchtime. No later."

Greco looked around the room. The others were busy, but had they heard? It would have to be McCabe first, and he wasn't looking forward to it. But he'd get the PM over with before he did anything else. Who to take?

"Joel, you will come with me to the Duggan this morning."

The young DC smiled. Despite the horror of it all, Greco knew that Joel wanted the experience.

Speedy shuffled on his chair. "What do you want me to do, guv?"

"The community centre. You and Leah go and speak to Clovelly. Find out who was there yesterday, and what Dee had been up to the past few days. We can rule out Max Marsh. He came here and then returned to the centre, where he stayed until late. Get hold of Dee's phone records too. After that, the forensic report on Ava Whitton's flat should be about ready. If not, chase it up. If there is anything interesting, let me know." Greco turned to Joel. "How did you get on with the houses that back onto that ginnel?"

"No one admitted to seeing anything, but one bloke was out. I'm going back later."

"Grace, take a close look at all the CCTV you can get hold of. Dee left here mid-morning. Where did she go? Did she meet anyone? We need answers. We also need to know who her family are."

"Uniform tried to find someone last night," Speedy told him. "She has a mother somewhere in Openshaw but they haven't been in contact for a while."

"Ask at the centre. Perhaps Clovelly will know."

"We've had an email from that DI at the drug squad," Leah told him. "You know, the one who thinks he can dictate the rules of the game. He wants a meet. What d'you think?"

"Okay — arrange it for later today. Ask him to come here."

Grace glared at him as he left the room, Joel in tow. "Lunchtime."

"Has Grace been ill, sir?" asked Joel. "Only, she looks very pale."

"You'll have to speak to her," Greco said. The last thing he wanted was to get into a conversation about Grace. He had other things to think about. He tossed Joel the car keys. "You can drive."

They badly needed a break on the case. As each day passed, things got more complicated. He'd no idea what Dee's murder meant. With luck, Bob Bowers would have something for them. If not, they would struggle.

\* \* \*

"Superficially, it looks the same as with Riley and Holt," the pathologist told them. "But in my opinion, it was rushed. I think your killer was either disturbed or was short of time. She was killed by a blow to the head. Whoever did it used a piece of rusty blunt metal. We found both rust and traces of motor oil embedded in the head wound. Her fingers were cut off after death, plus a number of heavy blows to the body were inflicted. Several bones were broken."

"Very similar to Craig and Vinny. Same killer or a copycat?" Greco asked.

Bob Bowers nodded. "Could be a copycat. The murder of those two lads has been widely reported. I read the gory details myself in one of the more salacious dailies. Reporters have collared anyone and everyone with a connection. I caught a couple of them harassing one of the cleaners yesterday."

At that moment, Roxy Atkins joined them. She was one of the centre's senior forensic scientists. "I have been running tests," she confirmed. "All three victims were drugged prior to death. Due to the state of Riley and Holt's bodies it is not possible to determine for certain how it was administered. But Dee Sampson's body was in fairly reasonable shape. We found a needle mark on her upper arm. She was injected with ketamine."

"She wouldn't just let someone do that," Joel pointed out.

"I agree," said Roxy. "The syringe was thrust hard into her arm, through her clothing, and it bled a lot. The two lads had also been given ketamine."

This suggested that it was the same killer. "What about Tomasz Bilinski?" Greco asked.

Roxy shrugged. "Decay is too advanced."

"How would our killer get hold of ketamine?" Joel asked Greco.

"It's easily available on the streets."

"He'd have to get hold of syringes too," Joel added. "Some chemists are a bit funny about selling them over the counter if you don't have a condition that needs injections."

Roxy had overheard him. "I am still running tests but I found the faintest trace of insulin in the injection wound. It is possible that your killer has access to insulin, or cares for someone who takes injections daily. Instead of disposing of the sharps properly, he has been hoarding some of them."

Greco thought about this for a moment. That information could be key. "Any idea what sort of weapon was used, other than being metal and oily?"

Bob Bowers shook his head. "I'm afraid not."

* * *

Speedy and Leah walked towards the centre entrance. "I'm getting sick and tired of coming here," he said.

"Don't antagonise Clovelly," Leah warned. "We need him onside. The kids trust him. We'll get nowhere without his help."

Max Marsh was in his room as usual. Graham Clovelly was talking to a group of youngsters in the café. The atmosphere in the place was sombre. They must have heard what had happened to Dee.

Graham stood up and came to meet them. "She didn't come here at all yesterday. I've spoken to everyone. Dee didn't talk about her personal life much. But she did tell Gina over there that she was seeing some bloke."

"Can we speak to the girl?"

Graham beckoned her over. "This is Gina, one of our regulars, and one of the community angels. If Dee had a best friend, then it was our Gina here."

"She kept some things secret from me," Gina said at once. "That bloke of hers, for instance. She wouldn't say who he was, or what he did. But she did bring him here once. He played pool with the lads. Stuck out like a sore thumb, he did. His clothes alone must have cost a fortune."

"Are you sure you don't know who he is?"

Gina looked at Leah. "She called him *Dom*, if that helps."

"Do you know where she was going yesterday?" Leah asked.

"To see you lot. Shit scared, she was. Reckoned you thought she stole that necklace. And she didn't. Marshy gave it to her like she said. I saw him. He was short of money. Dee gave him a couple of notes for it." Gina glared at them.

"Do you know if Dee ever saw her mother?"

"That old witch is a waste of space. Dee went round there a few weeks back, but all she got for her trouble was a mouthful of abuse. She was never up to much, even when Dee was little, so I've been told."

"Do you know where she lives?" Leah asked.

"The Crosslane Estate in Openshaw. You'll find her most nights in the Roebuck pub."

"Do you know where Marshy got the necklace from in the first place?" Speedy asked her.

"Look, I don't want to get anyone into bother."

"Dee was murdered, Gina. So were Craig and Vinny," he reminded her. "This killer has to be stopped, and we need your help."

Gina looked at Leah. She appeared to be weighing up her options. "Craig gave it to him," she said at last. "Payment for some favour or other." She backed away, raising her hands. "That's it. I've said enough."

"Get him over here," Leah told Graham. She'd had enough of being led around in circles. Max Marsh would tell them the truth or he'd spend a night in the cells.

"We thought he was holding out on us all along," Speedy told her. "Let's hope he finally sees sense."

"Sit down, Max," Leah instructed. The young man was edgy. He looked like he would make a run for it any minute. "Last chance, and you're bloody lucky to get one," Leah told him firmly. "It's time you told the truth. Why did Craig Riley give you that pendant?"

"Who said that?" he blustered. "They're lying to make trouble."

"We don't think so. So, come on, where did you get it?" Speedy asked.

Marsh appeared to be wrestling with what to say next. His eyes darted around as if seeking the answer in the room.

"Okay, I'll tell you," he said at last. "It was payment, but not for anything dodgy. Craig owed me." He fell silent, and looked from one detective to the other.

"Why did Craig owe you? What had you done for him, Max?" Speedy asked.

"I'm sick of this. You do someone a simple favour and it backfires for ever afterwards."

Marsh was evidently upset. His face was flushed and he kept flicking his hair off his face.

"What favour?" Leah asked. "If you know something, Max, then you must tell us. There is no guarantee that the killer will stop. I think he's covering his tracks now. Dee wouldn't talk to us, and look what happened to her."

Marsh looked at Leah and shrugged. "It was payment for getting him in with my group. Craig wanted to help, or so he said. He helped out in the room, setting up and the like. He got to know them all pretty well. They liked him. He could be a right laugh at times. Then, when they wanted stuff doing at home, Craig volunteered right away. I didn't see any harm. He was trying hard. He did some decorating for one of them and it mushroomed. He and Vinny were at it almost every day at one time." Marsh hung his head. "Now I realise what he was really up to. He and Vinny were robbing them blind."

"Anything else you're not telling us?"

"Dee didn't have anything to do with it. As far as I know she never went near any of their homes. She didn't think much of Craig or Vinny, either."

"It looks likely that she was involved in this somewhere, Max," Leah pointed out. "Otherwise, why was she killed?"

"Dee had friends she never spoke about. She earned money and never said how. She was secretive. She reckoned she was safer that way."

Speedy looked at him. "Well, she was wrong, wasn't she?"

# Chapter 21

By the time Speedy and Leah got back to the station, Greco and Joel were already back from the post-mortem.

"What have we got?" Greco asked them. He looked over to Joel, who was deep in conversation on the phone.

"Max Marsh finally came clean," Leah said. "The pendant was payment for letting Craig get pally with his group. They trusted Craig, let them into their homes. It seems likely it was a set-up. Once in there, Craig and Vinny helped themselves. Marsh says that he had no idea what was going on, and that Dee wasn't involved in the theft either. She never got that involved with the group. Also, her mother lives on the Crosslane. Perhaps we should get uniform to go and tell her. That place is worse than the Lansdowne."

Joel finally put the phone down. "That was a man whose flat overlooks the ginnel," he told them. "The one who was out before. He confirmed that he didn't see or hear anything. But he did say that the houses on the street where Dee was dumped are about to be refurbished. Alex Barton owns the lot. Plus, he owns one or two on the street behind — Balfour Street."

"That name again," Grace piped up. "It was Barton who Ava met in Manchester, don't forget. I checked her phone records, and there have been several calls made to Barton's office from her mobile. But even more to an unregistered mobile. Dee had also received calls and made them to that same number. I think both women know him, and Ava is doing business with him somewhere down the line."

"You think Barton is involved with the drug trafficking?"

"And the rest. He might appear whiter than white but that is a fairly recent thing. About ten years ago he was a well-known villain. The fact he was never caught and imprisoned was down to an expensive solicitor and damn good luck."

"Did you speak to those two girls?" Greco asked Leah.

"No, they never came round long enough to talk sense. I'll visit them both at home."

"Make it a priority," he told her. "Do we know if they overdosed or just had a bad reaction?"

"Could be either. The stuff they took was very strong," Leah replied.

"Grace, we'll speak to Barton. We'll try his office first."

\* \* \*

"You haven't said anything yet," Grace said.

"Give me chance. We've been mad busy all morning," Greco replied.

"I mean it, Stephen. You need to tell the team today."

"You still don't look well. Are you sure you wouldn't be better off at home?"

"I'm fine. Drop it."

"I'm only thinking of you — and the baby," he added as an afterthought.

"You don't get any better, Stephen. We're pregnant, we've both decided not to change that. You have to accept it. Tell the bloody team and get your head straightened out!"

\* \* \*

Barton's office was about a mile from the station. He had the top floor of a new block. The place was busy. He employed a number of staff. Barton's business certainly gave the impression of being above board.

"That unregistered mobile, you have the number?" Greco asked Grace as they got out of the lift.

"Added to my contacts, why?"

"I'll give you the nod and you ring it. It's taking a chance, but he might have the thing on him."

"Sneaky, Greco! That's not like you."

"We need to wrap this up. That stuff is dangerous and it's already hitting the streets."

They were shown into a room off the reception area. Alex Barton joined them after about five minutes.

"Sorry to keep you waiting," he said, and gave them an oily smile. "I can't think what we've done to merit the attention of the serious crime squad."

He was a big man with dark hair. Without the expensive clothes, he would look rough, intimidating. Greco made a mental note to look at his background when he returned to the station.

"You own a lot of property around the area," Greco began.

"It's what I do. I buy cheap, at auction mostly. Do the houses up, then either sell or let them. It's a profitable enterprise in the current climate. Plus, I'm providing a much-needed service for the community."

Greco ignored this. "You own properties on Balfour Street as well as the adjacent street."

"Yes, a recent major investment, and it's tied up a lot of cash. We won't see a return for several months.

However, it's better than allowing the houses to be demolished, wouldn't you agree?"

"A young woman was found dead around there. Were you aware of that?"

"How terrible! I had no idea." Barton looked from one to the other of them. "Nothing to do with my company, I hope? She wasn't trespassing, was she? Old properties can be dangerous places. We've done our best to cordon them off, but you know what these young folks are like."

"It wasn't an accident. It was cold-blooded murder," Grace said grimly.

"Like I said, awful. Who was it?"

"Somebody called Dee Sampson. Does the name mean anything to you?"

Barton seemed to be thinking. "Is she a tenant of mine? I don't think I've heard the name. But one of my staff can tell you if she rented property from us."

Barton was slippery. They needed to check the details and hit him with facts. "Do you know a woman called Ava Whitton?" asked Greco.

"No, I'm afraid not."

"That's very odd." Greco smiled. "You see, you met Ms Whitton in Manchester the other day. You drank coffee together and talked."

"I talk to a lot of people in the course of a day," Barton said. "What makes you think I know her?"

"She reckons you stole her purse," Greco told him.

"That's ridiculous. Why would I do that?"

"Who knows?" Greco looked at Grace.

Taking the hint, Grace took the mobile from her pocket and pressed the number. Seconds later, a phone rang in Barton's jacket pocket.

"Feel free to take that," Greco told him, still smiling.

Greco could see that Barton wasn't sure what was going on. Nonetheless he retrieved his phone and answered it.

"Mr Barton." Grace smiled.

"I'm afraid you are going to have to come down to the station with us," Greco told him. "You haven't been altogether truthful, have you? That phone you have was contacted on numerous occasions by both Ava Whitton and Dee Sampson. So, you see, Mr Barton, you do know who they are."

\* \* \*

Speedy had just taken a call from reception. "Barton's solicitor is here," he told the team.

"Speedy, you and I will interview him. Grace, take Joel and bring Ava Whitton in. If she's not at home, try Greysons."

"How do we see this going, guv?" Speedy asked as they strode along the corridor.

"I doubt he'll admit to anything. In fact, we'll be lucky to get the time of day out of him. He's a crook, and he's been a crook for a long time. He's trodden this path before, and knows how to come out on top."

Speedy sighed. "Not well, then."

"We have brought him in because of the calls back and forth between him and Dee and Ava. But we have no solid proof he harmed either of them. Call this an exercise in letting Barton know that we are on to him."

Alex Barton and his solicitor were deep in conversation when the two detectives entered the room.

The solicitor introduced himself. "I'm Harold Sackville. I represent Mr Barton."

Greco and Speedy sat down opposite the two men and Greco began.

"You have been brought here to answer questions regarding the death of Dee Sampson and the nature of your involvement with Ava Whitton. You can start by telling us how you knew Dee."

"She rented one of my flats. Ms Sampson often rang me to complain. Her latest beef was the boiler. Reckoned it was past it."

"We've added them up and there were eleven calls made by her to you over the past four days. Rather excessive, don't you think?"

"Not at all. That's what tenants are like. They keep on and on. They imagine I've got a magic wand."

"Ava Whitton," Speedy said. "How do you know her?"

"I've been thinking about that too. When you first mentioned the name, I had no idea," Barton said. "But now I realise that I do know her. She works at Greysons."

Greco nodded. "You have an involvement with that firm?"

"No," Barton responded. "But I have recently bought a piece of land adjacent to their premises on the Quays. Ms Whitton was very helpful when it came to certain questions I raised. The freeholders are notoriously difficult to get hold of. She was able to give me an alternative contact number. That's why I recognised her in town."

Plausible and irritating. The man had an answer for the lot. "You gave Ms Whitton your private number too?"

"Yes. I didn't see anything wrong with that. Have you met her?"

Greco nodded.

"Then you'll know that she's a very attractive young woman."

# Chapter 22

Speedy and Greco walked back to the incident room. "Slimy bugger, isn't he?" Speedy said.

"Yes, he's very good. He's obviously had sound advice off his brief. I was hoping he might say something that would give us the edge. But he didn't. We have no evidence, so we can't hold him. We will check him out thoroughly before we bring him in again. Find out about Dee's living arrangements. When we get Ava Whitton in here, we'll ask her about the land Barton was going on about."

A uniform came over to Greco when they entered the incident room.

"DI Grant Chambers is here, sir. I've put him in your office, hope you don't mind."

"Okay, I'll talk to him. Let me know when Grace and Joel get back with Ms Whitton," he told Speedy.

Grant Chambers was about Greco's own age. — tall, skinny and casually dressed in jeans. He sat at the desk with a cup of coffee.

"Thanks for agreeing to meet," Greco began. "We are working different aspects of the same case, I believe."

"We are investigating drug trafficking. You are not. We cannot allow you to muddy the waters. The people we are after must not suspect that we are on to them."

Greco nodded. He understood that well enough. "You do know that we have three murders on our hands? We can't just ignore them. I have just interviewed a person of interest. Drugs were not mentioned during the interview. However, we are aware that a large amount of heroin is behind those killings. To date, two young men and a young woman are dead. How they are mixed up in your investigation, I'm not sure. But the two do overlap. I also suspect that the deaths have something to do with a woman called Ava Whitton."

"You are right, she is involved. I doubt she has anything to do with the murders — not her style. The deaths will be down to the people she traffics for. She is responsible for bringing the stuff into the country. She works for a transport firm that goes regularly to Eastern Europe. What we don't know are the details."

Greco nodded. "You are talking about Greysons."

"Yes," said Chambers. "The lorries belonging to Greysons have been searched. Customs have visited the premises, but we have found nothing."

"Why her, and why is the fact Greysons go to Eastern Europe so important?"

"We had a tip-off about a year ago. A young man contacted us. He said he was Whitton's brother. He reckoned she was out of her depth and in danger. He wanted us to offer her protection. He gave us certain information that proved to be correct."

"Do you know what happened to that man?"

Chambers shook his head. "We haven't heard from him since."

"And you won't. His body was found in a ditch in a Cheshire field."

"In that case, they must have found out about the call. Based on what he told us, we launched a covert operation and put her under surveillance. We don't believe that Martin Greyson is involved, just Whitton. But she isn't working alone. She brings the stuff in and then passes it on. The problem is, we don't know how or who to."

"Did her brother tell you anything else?"

"He said he and others were being used as forced labour in Lincolnshire and East Anglia. Fruit picking, vegetable harvesting and the like. They were living in appalling conditions and being paid nothing. He said he was going to attempt to escape."

"He did, but they caught up with him," Greco said grimly. "Our investigations haven't thrown up very much that will help you. The three who are dead all went to a local community centre. We believe the two lads stole the heroin from Ava Whitton's house. They must have known it was there. But who told them is still a mystery. I doubt they are involved in the trafficking. They were simply opportunists."

"You have been very candid," said Chambers. "But we don't want your team involved in this."

"We are already involved. There is no way we can back out now. My job is to find who killed those young people. It is important to find the heroin, I agree. Some has already hit the streets."

"Do you have any clues as to where it is hidden?" Chambers asked.

Greco shook his head. "No. Apart from the tip-off, what makes you so sure that Ava Whitton is using Greysons' trucks to bring the stuff in?"

"Whitton's brother was adamant. He gave us her name and address. He told us to watch the shipments. He reckoned certain routes were key. I don't doubt he was right. There is a long supply chain. Most of the heroin originates from Afghanistan and is then moved on. The northern route runs from Bulgaria and Romania to Hungary, Austria, the Czech Republic, Poland or Germany, essentially by land. Hence the use of the lorries."

Greco frowned. "What I don't understand is if they are searched thoroughly, then surely you must find the stuff? It stands to reason."

"We have only the tip-off to go on. I have no doubt that he was telling the truth, but it isn't solid evidence. No one at Greysons will talk to us. We do not know which of the drivers are involved. We can't descend on every lorry of theirs that trundles off the ferry. Apart from which, they do not bring stuff in on every run."

"You have other methods. Technology, and dogs that sniff the stuff out."

Chambers grimaced. "We have found nothing."

"Have you heard of a local villain called Alex Barton?" Greco asked him. "Superficially he appears legit. Buys rundown property then sells or lets it. He might be worth looking at."

Chambers nodded. "His name has come up. But we could find no link between him and Whitton."

"We have found one. They contact each other regularly by mobile phone. He uses an unregistered one. Also, they met in Manchester earlier this week."

Grant Chambers made a note. "I don't want to step on your toes, but you have to understand our operation has been ongoing for months. Time and money have been invested in it. We believe we are close. You won't be allowed to jeopardise that, DCI Greco."

"With respect, DI Chambers, you are hardly close. You do not even know where on the trucks the drugs are hidden. Your searches have thrown up nothing. If Ava Whitton is involved, you have no idea who she passes the stuff to." Greco paused. He could tell from the look on his face that Chambers wasn't liking this one bit. "It is likely that my investigation will give you the answers you're looking for."

"No. You need to back off."

"Three murders? I don't think so."

"We'll see. My superior officer will be in touch." Chambers stood up.

Well, it had needed saying. This DI couldn't just come into Greco's station and lay down the rules.

* * *

DI Leah Wells pulled up outside the home of one of the girls who'd overdosed. Not the Lansdowne this time, but a semi in the leafy suburbs of Oldston. The girl's mother, the woman Leah had spoken to at the hospital, was sweeping the front path.

"Mrs Neville?" Leah asked.

The woman nodded, and immediately said, "Shona won't talk to me. I haven't gone on about what happened. I've said I don't blame her. Kids do all sorts of stupid things. I know I did. But I don't understand why she won't tell me how she got the stuff."

Leah looked at her notes. "Do you mind if I have a word?" It was possible that the girl was afraid of retribution if she said anything.

"Feel free. But be warned. Clammed up, she has. And I don't for the life of me know why."

Leah smiled at her and followed her inside. The house was neat and warm. Shona was sprawled on a sofa in the sitting room watching the TV. She didn't even look up when Leah entered and said hello.

Leah sat down. "I'm here about what happened to you and your friend. Do you know who you got the heroin from?"

The girl shrugged and cleared her throat. "Just some lad." Her eyes never left the TV screen.

"Does he have a name, this lad? Is he someone you see around?"

"Don't know."

Leah suspected that she knew very well who had given her the stuff. "How did you know he had stuff to sell? Did he approach you?"

Another shrug.

"Did you buy it off him?"

"No, he let us have it for nowt. Said we were an investment."

"He was hoping you'd get hooked. Want more," Leah explained. "The next time he would have charged you."

The girl shook her head. "I won't be trying it again. Made me feel like crap."

"This lad. Are you sure you don't know him?"

"No idea who he was. Just some lad hanging round the Lansdowne."

"You're not a stupid girl, Shona. You must see how unlikely that sounds. A strange boy approaches you, offers you drugs for no cost and you simply accept them?" Leah's voice now had an edge to it. "This is very important. People have died because of this. More people might too. If this stuff floods the area, then we're in trouble."

The girl finally looked at her. "They haven't died from the heroin. And me and Hazel are fine now."

"But you won't be the only ones this lad tempts with the stuff, Shona. Before we know it, a lot of people could become very ill."

"They won't."

"How can you know that?"

"I just do." Her gaze once more rested on the TV screen.

"Would you recognise this lad again?"

"Not sure. I might. But it was going dark and he was muffled up. He had a scarf wrapped round his face. Ask Hazel. She'll tell you the same."

Leah didn't doubt she would. The girls would have worked out their story together. They'd decided not to disclose anything useful, like names. But why? "Has anyone threatened you?" Leah asked. "Because if they have, they will be arrested and taken off the streets so that they are no longer a threat."

"No. I just don't know anything."

Leah left Shona and her mother to go and talk to Hazel. It was another wasted journey. Hazel Parker's story was much the same as Shona's. Leah was convinced that the two of them were hiding something. But what?

# Chapter 23

Grace had rung Greysons, only to be told that Ava Whitton was still off sick. Half an hour later, she and Joel were driving through the Cheshire lanes towards her house.

"Nice out here," Joel commented. "But they must cost a packet, these houses."

"Well, our Ms Whitton does alright for herself, doesn't she? Good job, profitable sideline in drug trafficking. She must be worth a fortune." Grace snorted.

"Not right though, is it? How come she's got away with it for so long?"

"She's a clever woman, and lucky. But I think her luck is about to run out. She's got both us and the drug squad on her tail now."

They pulled up outside the house. "I don't imagine she'll make a run for it, but just in case, be wary," Grace warned Joel as they walked towards the front door.

The blinds on all the windows were closed tight. Grace rang the doorbell and Joel banged on the window with his fist.

"The woman who lives there, she's not in." The next door neighbour came out into her front garden. "She left last night, bags packed, and got into a taxi."

"Do you know where she was going?" asked Grace.

"No. I'm afraid I don't really know her. A nod, a quick hello, that's about it."

She must have realised they were on to her. Grace rang the station and spoke to DI Leah Wells.

"I'll alert the airports and ports," Leah decided. "Mind you, if she left last night, she could be anywhere by now."

"I'll speak to the other neighbours, ma'am. See if anyone can add anything, but I doubt it. They are the 'keep themselves to themselves' variety around here. It might be worthwhile looking at the local taxi firms. Find out where she was taken."

"I'll get onto it," said Leah.

Joel stood looking up and down the road. "Thankless task. This is the sort of place where folk don't talk much. Houses are too far apart for a start."

Nevertheless, he and Grace went house to house on the small development. Most were out at work, but those who were at home knew nothing about Ava Whitton.

"We'll go to Greysons, see if any of her colleagues know her whereabouts."

"Why would she run?" Joel asked.

"Because we're getting too close. We spoke to Barton. If he is involved in the trafficking, she will have known. In all probability, Barton told her. But I bet the forensic search of her house was the final straw. She knew we'd find something, so she took off."

* * *

"Forensics are back about Ava Whitton's house," Speedy announced as soon as Greco returned to the incident room. "Traces of heroin in the utility room and in the boot of her car. Plus, fingerprints belonging to Riley and Holt all over the place. That settles it, sir. The two of them were definitely in that house."

Greco nodded. "Have we got anywhere with Ava Whitton's previous address?"

"Furnivall Street," Speedy told him. "And guess what? The house is owned by Alex Barton. She lived there for quite a while too. Got behind with the rent, according to the agency Barton uses."

"In hock to Barton. Not a pleasant situation to be in."

Leah joined them. "Grace has rung in. It looks like Ava Whitton has done a runner. The neighbours saw her leaving last night. Grace and Joel are off to Greysons, to see if anyone there can shed any light. A taxi firm in that area remembers her. The driver said he took her to Piccadilly railway station. She didn't say anything about where she was going, but she did have two suitcases with her."

Greco was annoyed. He should have foreseen this move by Ava. "Tell Grace to ask about that adjacent land, and to have a look at what Barton has done with it."

"We still need to speak to Callum Riley again, guv," Speedy reminded him. "Craig's death will still be raw, but we need to know what went on between the two of them."

Greco nodded at Speedy. "We'll do that." He turned to Leah. "Any luck finding Dee's mother?"

"I'm meeting her at the morgue. She has agreed to do the identification."

"We'll meet back here before we clock off. There is something I want to tell you all."

Speedy gave Leah a wink. "Go on, sir, give us a clue."

"You'll have to wait. I want Grace and Joel here as well. I'll have a chat with the super first."

Greco saw the looks, the curiosity on their faces. But McCabe had to be told first. He'd see him the minute they got back from the Lansdowne.

# Chapter 24

"Vinny Holt's mother is ill, I believe," Greco said.

"She spends most of her time in a wheelchair, sir," Speedy answered. "But I don't know what's wrong with her."

"Try and find out. I want to know why traces of insulin were in the needle mark on Dec's arm. It means we are looking for someone with diabetes. It's possible that Mrs Holt has it."

Speedy nodded. "That would put Dave Holt in the frame."

"It might, but it would depend on what evidence we can gather," Greco said. "How they dispose of the sharps would be a start. There is a procedure, but it would be a simple matter to keep some by."

The two detectives pulled up outside the Riley house. Speedy peered into a window. "Looks like they are in. I can see movement inside."

"We'll go easy. Craig's mother and brother are still grieving. We want Callum to talk to us. We don't want to antagonise him."

Mrs Riley let them in. She was calmer than last time. "I'm getting my boy back at the end of the week," she told them. "Apparently all the tests have been done. They won't tell me much about his death though. And they won't let me see him. Do you know why that is?"

Greco wondered what to say to her. He didn't want to upset the woman all over again. Telling her anything of the horrific detail would do exactly that. "It is best to remember your Craig as he was, Mrs Riley."

"I've read the papers. They wrote dreadful things. Said they'd both been beaten to a pulp and had their fingers torn off. Is that true?"

Greco tried to reassure her. "Both Craig and Vinny were heavily sedated first. It is likely that it was an overdose of the drug they were given that killed them. Whatever else was done to the lads was done after death."

She didn't reply, just turned and led them into the sitting room. It was small and cluttered. The furniture was too big, leaving little space. Four huge easy chairs and a large sideboard dominated the room. Every surface was covered in cheap ornaments, photographs and dust. It had the effect of making Greco uneasy and claustrophobic. Added to this, the Rileys had a dog, a large black thing that made Greco nervous. Its hairs were all over the furniture. The more he looked, the more Greco wanted to escape this place.

Speedy, on the other hand, didn't seem bothered. He flopped down onto one of the chairs and happily accepted the mug of tea Callum Riley offered him. Greco took his and placed it on a table. There was no way he would eat or drink anything in this place.

He turned to the young man. "Callum, tell me how you spent the day your brother was killed."

"I was at the community centre working in the food bank. It's open most days for a few hours, but on a Tuesday it's a full day's job. The vouchers are given out then, you see. I was mostly dealing with donations and putting stuff onto the shelves."

"Did you leave the centre at any time?"

"No, I arrived about nine thirty and it was gone six when I left."

"Did you see your brother at all?"

"No. The last time I saw Craig was the night before. The lazy sod was still in bed when I left for the centre that morning."

So far, his story chimed with what Graham Clovelly had told them.

"We're trying to build a picture of Craig's last days, what he was up to, who he spent his time with. Did he confide in you?"

"No. Craig didn't tell me anything. He thought I was soft. But he and Vinny were up to something. He was in his room and I heard him talking on his mobile. He was telling Vinny that he had the information, and they had to move fast. Whatever they were up to, they had a day to get it done."

The robbery in Handforth. "Do you know who Craig was in contact with?" Greco knew he could study the phone records, but that would take time. The heroin was already hitting the streets, so it was time they didn't have.

"I think it was some bloke called Dom. He came to the centre once. He knew Dee too. This Dom and Craig had a game of pool and talked a lot. He didn't fit in. He wore a suit and worked in some smart office on the Quays."

"Greysons?" asked Speedy.

"Yeah. I suspect it was Dom who got Craig the interview with them."

Greco nodded. "You've been very helpful."

"He's a good lad," his mother chipped in. Then she turned to Callum. "Get my eye drops when you go out. Bloody pain it is, losing your sight."

Greco looked at her. "Sorry, Mrs Riley?"

"Can't do anything about it. Part of my condition."

But Greco didn't want to get into a protracted description of all the woman's ills. "I'll keep you posted with events. Let us know if anything else occurs to you."

Outside the house, Greco hastily brushed down his clothes. "That place was filthy. I'll need a damn good scrub to get rid of the smell." Greco felt itchy, uncomfortable. Speedy on the other hand was fine. The case and events must be getting to him. His OCD was back with a vengeance.

"Just another family dwelling on the Lansdowne, guv." Speedy grinned. "Thought you'd be used to it by now."

"What did you think of Callum?" Greco asked. He was surprised at how cooperative Craig's brother had been this time. Maybe it was because his mother was there.

"Seems like an alright sort of lad. Why?"

"I'm not sure. What he told us, the way he related the events of that day sounded a little too practised to me."

"Clovelly backed him up. His alibi is sound."

"Handy that, don't you think? Grace and Joel, they've gone to Greysons. Ring Grace, and tell her to speak to this Dom. If he is in the least bit reluctant, get her to bring him in."

* * *

Grace flashed her badge at the receptionist. "We're looking for Ava Whitton."

"She isn't here. Off sick."

"Did she ring in?"

"I'll ask Mr Greyson to have a word with you."

Talking about Ava evidently made the young woman flustered. Grace had gone into the building alone, leaving Joel to have a prowl around the yard outside. She looked back through the large window and saw that he was eyeing up a tall wire mesh fence that separated Greysons from the land beyond.

"Is there a problem?" She hadn't noticed the man come into the reception area.

"Mr Greyson?"

He nodded. "We'll go into the office over here." He led the way to a small room off the reception. "Ava doesn't do sickness. In her time with us, I doubt she's had so much as two days off. This isn't like her, and I'm concerned."

"Why, Mr Greyson?" asked Grace. "It's winter. It is quite possible that she has succumbed to the flu, like most of the population at the moment."

"She's not been herself lately. She has been taking the odd hour off. Logged the time as dental appointments and the like. Something is going on."

"What do you think she is up to?"

Grace watched him ponder the question. He stared out of the window and his eyes widened. Joel.

"Is he with you?" Greyson asked.

Grace nodded.

"That land was sold recently. To a man called Alex Barton," Greyson said. "He says he wants it for a builder's yard. Apparently, he buys derelict houses and does them up. Ava knows him, but I don't know how. What I do know is that he is not a pleasant man. I have done some research, asked around. Barton is a crook. I think he has threatened Ava. I think she's in danger."

"That's quite an accusation. Do you have anything concrete to base it on?"

"I've seen them talking. She always seemed upset afterwards. He came round here asking questions when he first moved in. The ground is leasehold and he wants to build. He'll need the freeholder's permission, a simple matter. He didn't need to involve Ava. All it would have taken is a phone call to his solicitor. I don't for one second think that was what the visit was about. Ava was rattled. It was after that that she started to be absent from work."

"Customs and Excise were here. Has that happened before?"

"No, but everything was in order. I have excellent staff who do their jobs right. Dominic Hill dealt with them."

"Can I speak to him?"

Greyson picked up the office phone and made a call. A few minutes later, Dominic Hill entered the room. He was young, in his mid-twenties, good-looking and smartly dressed. He didn't look like the type of young man who would mix with the likes of Craig and Vinny.

Grace got straight to the point. "Tell me about your involvement with Craig Riley and Vinny Holt."

Dominic Hill smiled back at her and glanced at Greyson. "Sorry, I don't know them."

"Yes, you do. You were with Craig Riley at the community centre on the Lansdowne recently. If necessary, I'm sure we can get plenty of witnesses who will recall seeing you. Who else do you know there?"

The young man's face flushed. "Look, I don't know what this is, but I had nothing to do with the death of those two. I hardly knew Craig. We had a bit of business, that's all."

"That business involved a shedload of heroin and Ava Whitton, didn't it?"

Dom made a dive for the door but he ran straight into the arms of Joel Hough, who was just coming to join them.

# Chapter 25

"He's in the cells," Grace told Greco. "Dominic Hill is up to his neck in the heroin theft. You should have seen him when I mentioned it. As for the murders — difficult to tell. He knows about Craig and Vinny, and he's scared. But I don't think he knows about Dee. In the car coming back, he told me that he and Dee were close."

"He could be bluffing. We suspect that he was using her. She was his way in to the centre, and getting to know the others. I want his home searched."

"He has a flat in Gorton, above a shop on the High Street," Speedy told them.

"Owned by Barton?" asked Greco.

Speedy grinned. "How did you guess?"

"Hill knows both Ava Whitton and Barton, and he works at Greysons. Ideally placed, isn't he? Do we know if he sees anything of Barton?"

"No. When I mentioned the murders, he freaked," Grace said.

"Leave him to stew until we have the search results back," Greco said. "Where is Leah?"

"She's gone to see if she can find that friend of hers on the Lansdowne, sir," a uniformed officer told him. "Left about an hour ago."

That would be Roman, Greco thought.

"Report's in from forensics on the jewellery." Speedy had the document up on his computer screen. "Well, well, well. Plenty of prints, but none of them belonging to Max Marsh. His were only on the pendant. The ones on the other stuff all belong to Vinny and Craig."

Greco nodded. "In that case, it looks like Marsh was telling the truth."

The whole team had now assembled, including Leah, who had just come in. She looked his way and shook her head. So Roman couldn't help.

He couldn't leave it any longer. It was time to talk to McCabe about the baby. When he'd done that, he'd come and tell the team. "I'm just going to have a quick word with the super. No one leave until I get back."

Grace looked up from her desk and shook her head. "No need. I've told him."

Oh. She'd spoken the words so matter-of-factly. "Why did you do that? How did he take it?"

"Tell the others first," she said.

Greco was tongue-tied. He didn't know how to begin. Grace had gone behind his back and spoken to McCabe before he'd had the chance. He'd lost control of the situation again. That is, if he'd ever had it.

"Everyone!" he said too loudly. The nerves were back. Grace was looking at him, urging him on. "Grace . . . er, Grace and I want to tell you something." He fell silent, not sure if he could bring himself to do this. What would they think? Above everything else, he felt guilty, as though he'd let them all down.

"We're having a baby — him and me." Grace smiled, as if it was the most natural thing in the world. Despite this, the faces around them all wore bewildered expressions. "It's no big deal," she said. "Stephen and me, we're both pleased about it."

There was a long silence. Greco's throat was tight. He wanted to explain, but the words wouldn't come. Even if they did, what would he say? That this baby was the result of one drunken night in Brighton? He could hardly tell them that!

Finally, Speedy broke the silence. With a forced smile, he said, "Congrats to you both, I suppose."

Greco could see that his sergeant felt awkward. No doubt the others did too. This news would add a new dynamic to the team. Whether for good or ill, he didn't know. He wasn't even sure if he would still be allowed to work with Grace. For the time being, he did not want to think about their professional future. He was hoping she might prefer motherhood to the force.

"Thanks," he mumbled.

Leah smiled. "Well done, both of you. Any idea when?"

"Another six months yet," Grace said.

So that was how it would be. Baby talk for the foreseeable. Greco was thoroughly miserable. He went to his office and closed the door behind him. He needed time alone — to think.

* * *

Grace couldn't leave things as they were. Greco was obviously upset by the announcement. She got up from her desk, tapped on his door and entered. "I did you a favour, Stephen. You were never going to say anything, were you?"

He looked up at her. "You told McCabe. What did he say?"

"Wished us well, and suggested I get my maternity leave sorted so that he can look for a temporary replacement."

"I bet he's not so lenient with me. You're a member of my team, a detective constable. I got you pregnant. How does that look, Grace?"

She smiled. "It's not a crime, you know. I did make out that we'd been close for a while. I hope you don't mind. I thought that if McCabe saw us as a couple, it would be better all round."

Greco didn't blame Grace. In a way, she'd helped him out. He changed the subject. "Anything on the search of Dominic Hill's house?"

"I'll go and find out. Who do you want to interview him?"

"Myself and Speedy."

# Chapter 26

"He has the flat above the shop and the use of a garage. That's where we found it," the uniformed officer told Greco. "Wrapped in an old shirt and stuffed under the workbench."

The search had turned up a piece of thick metal pipe. It was grimy, oily and had blood and hair embedded in the rust on its surface. "Get that to the Duggan," Greco said. "We need to know if the blood belongs to any of our victims. It looks fairly fresh. It could have been used on Dee Sampson."

Speedy looked thoughtful. "Seems like Hill is our man. Did you find anything else? I'm thinking drugs, syringes, jewellery?"

The officer shook his head.

"So where is the heroin, sir? Where else might he hide things?"

"We'll be sure to ask him," Greco replied. "What about the shirt? Anything special?"

"Expensive, from one of those designer shops in the shopping centre on the Quays."

"Sounds like it could belong to Hill then," Speedy said.

Greco frowned. "Perhaps that's what we are supposed to think."

The two of them hurried along the corridor and down the stairs to the cells. Greco asked for Hill to be brought to an interview room.

"You and Grace, sir. Going to make a go of it?"

Now, *there* was a question. If he answered in the negative, Speedy was sure to tell her, and that would cause upset. Greco didn't want that. "More than likely." He forced a smile.

"You surprise me. I didn't realise the pair of you were so full-on. Grace, yes, she's liked you from the off. But it has taken you a while to catch up, hasn't it?"

Greco held up his hand. "Not now. This isn't for discussion at work." The truth was, Greco couldn't discuss it. The subject of Grace and the future was difficult, and fraught with problems. He'd only just told the team, but already the whole thing was making him feel trapped. Baby or no baby, he couldn't help wishing that things were very different. And the last thing he needed was to be the butt of smutty jokes in the office.

Dominic Hill was brought in. He sat down opposite the two detectives.

"Do you want a solicitor?" Greco asked him.

"I don't need one. I haven't done anything," he said. "I have no idea why I'm even here."

"You work for Greysons," Greco said. "What exactly do you do there?"

"I didn't know working there was a crime," Hill replied nervously. "I work for Ava Whitton. She is the transport manager."

"Ms Whitton is currently missing. Do you know where she is?"

Hill shook his head. "She could be anywhere. I think she's done one. Things have got tricky."

"Would you tell us what you mean by that, Dominic?" Greco asked.

"I know why you've brought me here. You think I had something to do with Craig and Vinny being killed." He looked at them, his expression defiant. "Well, I didn't. I didn't even know them very well."

Greco returned his look. "I asked you about Ms Whitton. What do you know about her part in all this?"

Hill shook his head.

"Craig and Vinny robbed Ms Whitton's house. They stole money, jewellery, and a lot of heroin that was hidden there." Greco paused, giving Hill time to think about this. "It's our belief that Greysons' lorries are used to bring the stuff into the country. And I think the lads knew exactly when to strike. In effect, they were tipped off. You see, it happened the very day that Customs and Excise did that spot check on Greysons' premises. Odd, don't you think? Either that or bloody good luck."

Hill was staring at his hands. "I didn't think it would do any harm," he said quietly. "I've been watching Ava for a while. I suspected what she was up to. She's not as smart as she thinks. She panicked that day, made mistakes. Got away with it by the skin of her teeth. She has to be mixed up with some right dodgy types. They will be looking for her. I'm not surprised she's disappeared."

"Why Craig and Vinny? Why get them involved?" Greco asked.

"Dee told me about them. I thought if we got our hands on the heroin we could get money off Ava in return for giving it back. She would pay through the nose to save her skin. She'd have no alternative. She knew the consequences of letting certain people down."

"Which people, Dominic?" asked Greco.

Hill was pulling at his fingers, frowning. Finally he looked up. "Barton. He is at the bottom of this. Ava brings the stuff in, and he moves it on."

"You're sure of this?"

"Yes."

"How? I imagine it's not information Barton or Ava would volunteer."

"I'm on Barton's payroll. He trusts me. Well, up to a point. In my position I can both hear and see things."

"Can you prove what you're telling us?"

"No, not really. Whenever Barton has discussed things, there's been no one else around. If it came down it, it would be his word against mine. But if it's all the same, I don't want it to come to that. He's a scary bugger. Barton would make sure I never said anything again!"

"Tell us about Craig and Vinny," Greco said.

"I couldn't have done this on my own. Dee introduced us and we made plans. We had no intention of selling the stuff. I don't know about those lads, but I wouldn't know where to start. We were going to get Ava to pay a ransom to get it back. I met them at the community centre, and we organised things."

"So, what happened?" Greco asked. "Because something went radically wrong."

"I'd had a tip-off that Customs and Excise were going to visit so I told the lads to be ready."

"Who told you this?" Greco asked.

"An anonymous phone call one night when I was working late."

"And you believed it?"

"I had no reason not to. If it was a hoax, that was just our bad luck. I told the lads straightaway. That morning I rang Craig and they went to Ava's house. They found the heroin okay, rang me and we arranged to meet later that night. But they never turned up. I was angry. I presumed they'd made off with the stuff. Cut me out of the deal."

"Where were you supposed to meet?"

"The old mill on Bentinck Street. It's empty and has a large yard. No one goes there. We were going to hide the heroin, then tap Ava for the money."

Greco thought about this. Hill had admitted to his part in the robbery, inasmuch as he passed on vital information, but could he be believed about the rest? "Did you turn up?"

Hill nodded. "It was a wet night and dark, but no one had been there, I could tell. No tyre marks in the mud, only mine. I waited about an hour and gave up. I had a look around the local pubs, but couldn't find them."

"You know Dee Sampson?"

Hill nodded.

"You were close?"

"I like Dee. I've taken her out a couple of times. It was her who took me to the centre to meet the lads. Mind you, she didn't know what we were planning."

"Dee played no part in your scam?"

Dominic shook his head. "No."

"Dee Sampson was found battered to death earlier today," Greco told him. "Her murder was similar to that of Craig and Vinny."

Hill's eyes opened wide with shock. He shook his head slowly. "I don't understand. Why her? Why go after Dee?"

"We have no idea. Are you sure she wasn't involved in any way?"

"She introduced us, me and the lads. Nothing else."

"While you've been here, we have carried out a search at your home. We found something in your garage. The weapon used on Dee. It's on its way to the lab. Is the blood on what we've found going to match Dee's?"

"I had no idea that Dee was dead!" Hill shouted. "And I certainly didn't kill her. Why would I? I liked Dee. We'd just started seeing each other. Anyway, I'd been at work all day. Then I got arrested."

He was right. Dee had been murdered in the early afternoon, not long after she left the station. But if Hill hadn't killed her, who had?

Greco decided they could go no further for the time being. "That's all for now. In view of what we've found, you might want to reconsider having a solicitor present the next time we talk."

"I've told you everything I know. Can I go now?"

"I'm afraid not, Dominic. You will be staying with us for a while longer," Greco said.

# Chapter 27

Day 7

The journey to Poland had been a long, hard slog. But at least now he was in his homeland, Vasili Pakulski could speak to people and understand what was being said. Now it was George Potts' turn to be at a disadvantage.

They had delivered the goods and were on their way back to Calais with a truckload of tinned food destined for a Polish wholesaler in Manchester.

A couple of hours out of Warsaw, Potts suddenly announced, "We're pulling into a workshop for a while. Something on the truck needs checking out. Use the time. Get something to eat or go for a walk."

Potts pulled off the main road and down a country lane. Vasili had no idea what was going on, and Potts was evidently in no mood to tell him. The truck seemed fine. Vasili was no expert, but there didn't seem to be anything wrong.

The workshop was a ramshackle affair, way off the beaten track. The man who ran it gave Potts an unenthusiastic greeting, and spoke to him in broken English. "Same as before?" he asked.

"Make it quick. I want to get going," Potts barked.

The man swore in Polish and Vasili smiled to himself. George Potts didn't understand. But he deserved it. He wasn't a nice man.

Potts walked off towards the workshop.

"There is a drinks machine inside," the mechanic told Vasili.

"Thank you. I'll get a coffee," he responded in Polish.

The mechanic broke into a smile and clapped him on the back. "When you're ready, you can help me if you want. The work is heavy and that one just sits around on his backside." He nodded at Potts, who by now was sitting outside on a bench, smoking.

"What's wrong with the truck?" Vasili asked the mechanic.

"Nothing. It is just the usual job."

Vasili was curious. He had no idea what this was about. He stood back and watched the mechanic remove the second diesel tank from the side of the truck.

"What's your name?"

"No names — not real ones anyway." He raised a finger. "But you can call me Kovac. Don't tell him. That man is the scum of the earth. His attitude stinks."

"This is my first time with him, and I hope I never have to do this again."

"Get out while you can, my friend. They are evil, the lot of them. I am like you. I need the money. I owe them, and if I refuse to do what they ask, my family will get hurt. They have killed people. I have seen some horrific things. What's your story?"

"If I don't work for them, we lose our home. They were going to throw us out onto the streets. I badly need to find somewhere else to live. Then I will be gone."

Kovac started to manhandle the heavy tank. "Give me a hand to carry this inside. They are bad men, yes, but this is very clever." Once they were inside the workshop with the tank on the bench, Kovac pushed a dipstick into the tank's filler hole. He held the stick up to the light. "What do you see?"

"Fuel," Vasili responded, and smelled it just to make sure.

"Diesel, exactly, my friend. But all is not what it seems." Kovac took an electric saw to one end of the rectangular tank and cut it clean off. Now Vasili could see inside. The filler hole opened up into a small container. The rest of the tank was filled with bundles of used notes. Vasili had never seen so much money. He reckoned there must be thousands in there.

"Help me get it out," Kovac instructed.

The two men hauled the bundles onto the bench, a handful at a time.

Vasili said nothing. He felt queasy. This was bad. They had travelled from the north of England with all this money on board. But what he saw next made him even more nervous.

Kovac took a large cardboard box from a shelf. He opened it up and passed Vasili a see-through plastic packet containing white powder. The box contained dozens more just like it. "We must pack the goods in tight. Do not worry. He has done this many times before." He nodded at Potts. "We fill up the tank with the drugs, and I weld it back together. Simple and efficient." The last three words were spoken in English.

"And foolproof." Potts came up behind them. "Customs get nosy, they fiddle about with the tank and find nothing but diesel. The dogs don't find it because of the smell. The fuel goes into that small container." Potts pointed. "Then this tank is fitted into a bigger one, forming an outer shell. That way customs do not see the weld. We top up the space between the inner and outer shell with more diesel and fool the bloody mutts."

It was only now that the full impact of what Vasili had got himself into, hit him. His stomach churned. This was drug trafficking on a huge scale. If he did nothing, went along with this, then he too was a criminal, every bit as guilty as Potts and whoever he was working for. Vasili could not live with that.

* * *

Ava Whitton was unrecognisable. The gloss was gone, replaced by trainers, ripped jeans, a hoodie and a rucksack. Her hair was now almost black, and hung in a straight bob to her chin.

She had travelled south, and taken a room in a cheap hotel room near Cannock in Staffordshire. Sometime soon, the Greysons' lorry she was waiting for would roll by. There was a scheduled stop — a motorway café on the M6. All Greysons traffic stopped there and checked in with the office. Their arrival time was reported back at base. Potts and his co-driver would take a break there. That is when she'd strike.

Ava had a plan, of sorts. But it was by no means foolproof. Not her usual style, but she'd had to move quick. She would need help. The lorry she was waiting for would be driven by Potts. She was hoping that his sidekick, Vasili Pakulski, the man she'd hired a few days ago would help her. He was Polish, like her, and had been coerced into the job by Barton. By now he would be aware of what was really going on. If he had any conscience at all, he would do as she asked.

It was Ava's plan to take the lorry, get Vasili Pakulski to drive, and to leave Potts behind. They would take the lorry north, and lure Barton to a meeting place. She didn't know what she'd do after that. Ava wanted Barton dead, but she wasn't a killer. But if she didn't kill him, she would have to get the police involved. To send Barton away, she would have to provide the evidence they would need.

* * *

Vasili and Potts were making good time. They would reach the port of Calais before nightfall. Vasili had sat in silence since leaving the workshop and Kovac behind. He couldn't get what he'd seen out of his head. They were shipping drugs into the UK. He could not simply sit back and let that happen. The heroin was destined for the streets. It ruined lives. He had to tell someone. But if he did that, what would happen to his family? One whiff of the police, and Barton would throw them out onto the streets. And that was the very least he'd do. They would never be safe. Barton would take revenge. He had to warn Nadia and his daughters.

"When we stop?" he asked Potts in broken English.

"I'll pull in at the next café," he said. "Then it's a straight run through to Calais. And no whining. Got it?"

Vasili nodded. "How long?"

"Half an hour. You'll just have to wait."

Vasili settled back and closed his eyes. Potts was singing his head off to the music on the radio. It was wearing him out. They had gone the entire journey and, so far, Potts had done all the driving. Vasili began to wonder what he was doing here at all. He didn't see what he was needed for.

"You want me to drive?" he asked Potts.

"No."

"Then why I here?"

"To ride shotgun." Potts laughed. Then he nodded to the glove compartment.

Vasili opened it and rummaged around. Potts hadn't been joking. Inside, hidden behind a couple of drink cartons, was a pistol. "You can't expect me to use that. I not shoot anyone."

"You'll do as you're told. We meet trouble, you use the gun. Refuse, and Barton will punish you."

"Killing not right."

Potts grinned. "These roads aren't always safe. But don't worry. Shoot somebody and we don't leave any evidence behind. You won't get caught."

# Chapter 28

Greco arrived at the station early the next morning. He was alone in the incident room. He wanted time to sift through the reports and weigh up what they had. At first he had been certain that Dominic Hill was their man. But now Greco knew that couldn't be. The young man had an alibi, for starters. He'd told them he was at work until he'd been arrested. That needed checking out. But Greco doubted the young man was a killer. Someone had set him up. But why? And more important, who?

He stared at the board. Why had the killer labelled the bodies? Care had been taken to ensure that whoever found the lads knew who was who. Then there were the body parts. Everything was there. It was almost as if the killer cared.

The team were assembled and at their desks before eight. Even Grace was in bright and early. She still didn't look well, but she would not appreciate any special attention.

"Have we got anything new?" Greco asked them.

"I spoke to the two girls who overdosed," said Leah. "They are hiding something. Both reckon they do not know whoever gave them the heroin. That's unlikely. They know right enough. But for reasons of their own, they won't say."

"Why not?" Grace asked.

"I thought at first that they might be afraid. But that's not it. There is something else, I'm sure of it."

"See them again," Greco suggested. "Keep pushing."

"Any word on Ava Whitton?" asked Speedy.

"Nothing. Ports, airports and railway and coach stations have all been alerted," Joel replied. "But so far, no one has seen her."

"Are we keeping tabs on her mobile?"

Speedy nodded. "If she uses it, we'll know. But nothing so far."

"We still have Dominic Hill in the cells." Greco looked at Joel. "Get onto the Duggan. We need the results from the iron bar."

"Has he offered an alibi?" Grace asked.

"Yes. He told us he was at work. That is probably true. Speedy, get on it straight away. Check with Greyson. Make sure Hill didn't leave at any time. If Hill's alibi does check out, it gives us another problem."

"How, sir? Apart from the obvious one that we've lost our only suspect?" Speedy asked.

Greco looked at all of them. "Think about it. Evidence was left for us to find. If that bar is the murder weapon, then the real killer is trying to frame Hill."

Speedy scratched his head.

"See anything of Dee on the CCTV from the immediate area?" Greco asked Grace.

"She can be seen leaving our building. From there she appears to be heading for the bus stop. It was raining, remember. The camera we really need is on the corner of Hampson Street. But it was out. So we lose her at that point." Grace shrugged.

"I've been thinking about the way Craig and Vinny were found. Any ideas on that, anyone?" He looked at

172

them. "What I'm getting at is writing their names on the bodies, leaving the amputated parts with them."

"Does it have to mean anything?" Speedy asked.

"Perhaps someone cared," Leah suggested, echoing Greco's own thoughts. "Wanted to make sure we got the identities right."

"But why?" Speedy said. "We would have found out soon enough. Both boys' DNA is on record."

"Perhaps we shouldn't even try to analyse the thoughts of our killer, sir," Joel suggested. "Who knows what goes on in such minds?"

Greco nodded. "Fair enough. I don't know what it means. But I do think the way they were left is significant. Another aspect we have not looked at properly is why the beatings and the thing with the fingers." He looked at Leah. "Do some digging, will you? Perhaps speak to Roman again. Ask if there's been anything else like this."

Leah nodded.

Joel Hough was tapping at his computer keyboard. "The report is through from the Duggan, sir. It was Dee's blood on that bar. Ms Atkins reckons the rust flecks are from the piece of metal that was used on Craig and Vinny too."

Greco's face pulled into a frown. "Same killer, then."

* * *

Martin Greyson was angry. "Half my bloody staff is missing! What the hell's going on? Ava went walkabout days ago and now you lot have made off with Dom."

"Can't be helped, Mr Greyson," Speedy told him. "As for Ava Whitton, we've no idea where she is. But be assured, we are looking for her. Your other employee, Dominic Hill, is helping us with our enquiries."

"Rubbish! Dom's not done anything. He's too much of a chicken."

"Can you confirm where Dominic was yesterday?" Speedy asked him.

"He worked here all day. Until you lot came and carted him off, that is. Damn shame. We had stuff to discuss. What with Ava being missing, I'm considering making him up to transport manager, temporary, like."

"And you're sure he didn't leave? He didn't take half an hour to go somewhere?"

"No. Most of the day he was working in my office, with me. When he wasn't there he was at his desk. Half a dozen others can confirm that too."

As soon as he was outside, Speedy rang Greco and told him. "Hill's alibi checks out. He isn't our killer. So what now?"

"Our killer is trying to set him up. He knows him. Knows Hill and Dee were close. I'll speak to him again."

* * *

Greco smiled at Hill. "You were telling the truth about Dee's murder, Dominic. We no longer suspect you of killing Dee. But all the same, you are not completely innocent. You were complicit in a robbery. The heroin you helped to steal is bound to hit the streets. Some already has, and the users had to be hospitalised."

"It was about quick cash, that's all," he said. "That, and getting one over on Barton."

"You don't like Alex Barton?"

"He's a crook and a bully. He terrified Ava. I'm on his payroll, but that doesn't mean I'm any sort of favourite. Cross him and you're dead." Hill leaned forward and fixed his eyes on Greco. "My life won't be worth shite when I get out of here. He'll have me picked up and given the third degree. It'll be my body you're scraping off of the pavement next."

"Then help us, Dominic, and we'll protect you. We want Barton, but we need evidence."

Greco watched the young man consider this.

Finally, Hill shook his head. "No. He'll kill me. You think you can protect me, but you can't. He has people everywhere. You have no idea what that man is capable of, or what he does to those who cross him. He gets wind of my part in stealing the heroin . . . I've heard things. Barton and his minions talking, boasting about what they've done. I don't know who killed Craig and Vinny but they were tortured first. They had their fingers hacked off. Typical Barton, that is. Tells everyone it's what he does to any light-fingered chancer who steals from him."

"The beating, the finger down the throat, that's a Barton trademark?"

Hill nodded. "Doesn't get his own hands dirty, mind you. Gets one of his mob to do it for him."

"Do you know anything about him using forced labour?"

"Yes. He sends the poor buggers down south to work the fields. Object, or try to escape, and you get the same treatment. He doesn't pay them either. The farmer pays Barton though, but he keeps it for himself."

That must have been what happened to Ava's brother, Tomasz Bilinski, Greco mused.

"You had better stay with us a little longer," Greco told him. "Purely for your own safety. In the meantime, who else did you tell about Barton's methods?"

"The lads knew. I've no idea who they told."

# Chapter 29

Ava left the guest house and took a taxi to the motorway service station. She bought a coffee and settled down in a window seat. From here she would see the Greysons' lorry pull in. She was nervous. There was only one shot at this. Mess up, and Potts would contact Barton. That would mean the end. There would be no second chance.

She knew that once they arrived, Potts would make for the café. That was her opportunity to speak to Vasili Pakulski on his own and convince him to help her. He had been forced into this because of circumstances. Ava hoped he would grab this chance at freedom with both hands.

She hunkered down on her seat. The disguise, plus large sunglasses covering most of her face meant that there was no chance of being recognised. She checked her watch frequently. It should not take more than two to three hours to get from the ferry port to here.

The traffic report came on the café radio. Traffic was heavy. More waiting. The nerves were making her feel sick. It was today or never. She would not get another shot at this. Get this wrong, and Barton would win. Ava didn't want that.

After an agonising wait, the lorry finally pulled into a parking bay. Ava watched them get out of the cab. The two men didn't talk to each other. Potts was whistling. He made off on his own without even looking back at Vasili. Typical of the man. The only person he got on with was Barton.

Potts walked towards the café. Once he had joined the queue at the counter, Ava ducked into the ladies, and then out by the rear exit. Vasili Pakulski was on his mobile, still standing by the vehicle.

Ava threw a quick glance back through the café window and spotted Potts. He had a large plate of breakfast in front of him, and was busy stuffing his face. She still had Pakulski's number on her mobile. She waited for him to finish his call then tapped it in. It was risky. The police would be monitoring her calls. But she had to speak to him. They had to talk, but out of sight of prying eyes.

"Vasili, it is Ava," she began in Polish. "I gave you the job, remember? I must talk to you. Say nothing to anyone, particularly not to Potts. Meet me around the back of the main building, by the rubbish bins."

Ava had done her homework. She knew the layout of this place like the back of her hand. She knew that no one in the café could see them there. She closed her eyes and prayed. *Please don't tell Potts. Please don't tell Potts.* The words kept running through her head. Minutes later, Vasili approached her. He didn't look happy.

"It was you who got me into this! You should have warned me about these people! They are crooks, criminals. They trade in drugs. Now I am no better than them," he hissed at her.

"I'm sorry, Vasili," she replied in Polish. "But you are not a criminal. You were forced into this. Barton would have put you and your family on the street if you had not agreed to work for him. Possibly worse. He is a hard man. I am in the same position as you, but for different reasons. But if we work together, we can both be free."

"How can we do that?" Vasili scoffed. "Potts won't allow anything to go wrong. He is an animal. There is a fortune in that lorry. Do you know he even has a gun in the glovebox?"

That didn't surprise Ava. She also knew that he would not hesitate to use it.

"You picked up the drugs? Nothing went wrong at customs?"

Vasili nodded. "Everything was smooth. One of the diesel tanks is stuffed with heroin. You and Barton have turned me into a very bad man. If we are caught, I will go to prison. What will my family do then?"

"I will do my best to ensure that does not happen," she assured him. "I am afraid of Barton too. He wants me dead. You have to help me, Vasili. We must help each other. Please, we need to do this. If we succeed, you and I will both be free. Barton won't threaten or harm us anymore. You will have money too."

\* \* \*

Greco reported back to the team. "What was done to Craig and Vinny was typical Barton, so Dominic Hill tells me. We could do with knowing who, outside of his immediate circle, knew that."

"It can't be common knowledge or Roman would have known," Leah said. "But currently nothing is known about Barton other than that he is whiter than white. The official story is that he is a reformed character. A businessman. A man of the people, who provides cheap housing for the needy. Sounds almost saintlike, doesn't he?"

"The fingers thing is his trademark punishment for those who steal from him. We were meant to believe that Barton was behind the killings," Greco said.

"Pushing it a bit, guv, given that no one knows about this trademark." Speedy shrugged. "Perhaps we should let the truth get out."

Greco ignored Speedy's comment. "Hill said he told the lads. They could have told someone else, the killer for example. Whoever our killer is, he couldn't carry out the killing with the same brutality as Barton. All the mutilation took place after they were dead."

"Perhaps he couldn't bring himself to do it," said Leah. "Perhaps he knew them, and found he did care after all. Not that that gets us anywhere. We're still none the wiser."

Greco sighed. "We'll go through the details again. Ava Whitton's internet usage. Where is her laptop?"

"The Duggan have it, sir," Joel replied.

"Find out what she used it for," Greco said.

"Do we have any idea yet of anybody who is insulin dependent?" Joel asked.

"Not Vinny Holt's mother, despite being in a wheelchair most of the time," Speedy said.

"Do more digging. The killer got those insulin-contaminated syringes from somewhere."

"What about Barton?" Grace asked. "Hill has labelled him the killer, and told us about the man's MO, so why are we waiting?"

"Evidence, Grace. We need cast-iron proof before we can go near him. Hill has heard plenty, but that's it. Words, but no substance."

"I'll go and have another word with those girls today," Leah said. "It is vital we know who gave the heroin to them. Though interestingly, no more of it has hit the streets."

Leah had a point, Greco realised. Someone was sitting on a fortune, so what was stopping them?

Joel was looking through the online reports from the Duggan. "Nothing in yet about the laptop," he told the team.

"Ring them," Greco suggested. "Go down there if necessary. That laptop might hold the evidence we need. The damn thing wasn't kept for its ornamental value."

# Chapter 30

Alex Barton scrolled through the contacts on his mobile and tapped on Martin Greyson's number.

"Martin! I was supposed to have a meeting with Ava this morning. She didn't show. Is she okay?"

"There is nothing in her diary," Greyson replied. "What did you want to see her about? Perhaps I can help instead."

"We have recently been talking about your firm doing some work for me. I often need to ship building materials about the country. We planned to discuss the details over coffee."

There was a silence. Barton assumed that Greyson was considering this.

"She never mentioned it to me." More silence. "I'll tell her you called."

"Is she there?" Barton asked. "I really do need a word."

"Sorry, Mr Barton, Ava is tied up with something at the moment. I will tell her you rang. I'm sure she'll get back." Greyson ended the call.

"The bitch is avoiding me. And that boss of hers is covering for her. Do we have someone at her house?" Barton looked up at the individual towering before him. He was a giant of a man, well over six foot, and heavily built. His fair hair was all bristle, cut close to his scalp. "I want her found, Archie. She owes me. When I catch up with her, Ava Whitton will rue the day she tried to cross me."

"The house is being watched, sir," Archie replied. "But there has been no movement for days. There's no one there."

"The bitch is not at work either, I'd stake my life on it. Greyson is lying to us."

\* \* \*

The IT technician looked up at Joel from the laptop. "She used it for one purpose only. And she only ever visited one site. It had been set up on the dark web to administer the comings and goings of drug shipments. Ava Whitton logged what money was sent, and what drugs came back. Think of it as bookkeeping for traffickers."

"Can you tell me who else had access to the site?"

"That is tricky. A series of passwords are used, and the IP address can't be traced. But I do know that more people than just Ava had access to it."

"Everyone involved entered their piece of the jigsaw."

"Yes, I'd say so. At any given time, the movement of the drugs and money could be traced."

"Interesting, but not much use for evidence purposes." Joel grimaced. "We really need a break on this one. Is there nothing you can do?"

"Other people used the site. If you could get hold of other devices that accessed it, that would be proof."

That got Joel thinking. One of the people who was bound to have kept tabs was Barton. Depending on how savvy the man was, he might even have used the site from his mobile phone.

181

Joel rang the station and told Greco what he'd learned.

"All very useful," the DCI agreed. "But before we can lay our hands on Barton's stuff, we have to have evidence for the warrant."

"There is something," the technician called out to Joel as he ended the call. "There's a lorry due in at any time. According to the log, it will have come through Dover early this morning."

* * *

"You are in no position to make such promises, Ms Whitton," Vasili said. "And how do we square your appearance with Potts?"

"You forget, Vasili, it was me gave Potts a job in the first place. I doubt he knows anything about my problem with Barton. Apart from which, he won't recognise me," Ava said.

"He knows you better than me," Vasili warned. "What do you intend to do?"

"We must disable Potts, take his phone, and get the keys. You will drive the truck north, and I will arrange to meet Barton."

"What then? Provided your plan works, what do we say to Barton? He won't want to talk. He will want his drugs."

"That is my problem, not yours. Once we reach our destination, you are free, Vasili. I will deal with Barton alone."

Vasili was silent for a moment. "You will kill him?"

"I'm not sure. I want to, but I'm not a murderer."

"You could hand him over to the police. You have evidence that will incriminate him?"

Ava nodded. "We have to move quick. Potts won't be long. Go and find him. Tell him there is a problem with the truck."

"What problem?"

"Tell him that some kids have been trying to get inside. That should rattle him."

Vasili walked off towards the café and minutes later, returned with Potts.

"You're here to deal with problems like this," Potts grumbled. "Do I have to do everything?"

Vasili led him to the back of the vehicle. "They have tried the rear doors. Look, they have damaged one of them."

"Bloody hell!" Potts cursed. He stood facing the doors, fumbling with the lock and pulling on the handle. "Can't see anything wrong. I left half a mug of tea to—"

Ava struck. She lunged at him with a cosh, hit the back of his head, and sent him staggering to the floor. He lay still for a few seconds, then he groaned and tried to get up. The look on his face was thunderous. Ava panicked. She had never been violent. This was way out on a limb for her.

"Hit him!" Vasili screamed. "For God's sake, hit him again!"

Ava didn't know what to do. She threw the cosh to Vasili and closed her eyes. She dare not look, but she heard the dull thuds as Vasili hit him several more times.

"You haven't killed him?" she exclaimed.

"No, but he is well out of it."

"We must get him inside, then tie him up," she told Vasili. "Get the keys."

Potts was heavy, and they didn't have long. Fortunately, he had done his usual thing of parking some distance from anything else.

Between the two of them, they managed it. Potts' wrists and ankles were tied tight with a length of packing tape. He was gagged and tethered to a metal strut inside the lorry. Ava fished in his pocket and took his mobile.

# Chapter 31

Joel was back at the station. "I was thinking on the way here. There are CCTV cameras the length and breadth of the motorway system, sir. If they caught the lorry, we could stop it, have it searched."

"That's a big 'if,'" Greco said. "There is a lot of motorway out there, and they are travelling at speed." Nonetheless, he had to consider the idea. They had nothing else. Ava was involved, and according to Hill, so was Barton. If the cameras did pick up the lorry, at least it was a step nearer. He made his decision. "We'll get a warrant organised. Get onto Traffic. Set up the watch on the motorways. The minute that lorry is spotted, I want to know. Contact Greysons, find out what they've got out there today, and the direction of travel."

Within half an hour, Joel had a list of all Greysons' lorries currently on the roads.

"Three are in the north, either going to or returning from Scotland. One is making its way down to Dover. A shipment of engineering parts destined for Poland. And one is on its way back to base. It's returning from Warsaw with a shipment of tinned food. It came through the port of Dover earlier today."

"That has to be the one," Greco said.

"Ava Whitton has used her mobile!" Speedy called out excitedly. "I have been onto her provider and had the GPS turned on, so we can track whoever she calls. The tech boys have got the number she rang. It's not one that's known to us. They are tracing the owner now." Speedy sat at his computer, staring at a map on the screen. He pointed. "Here. Whoever owns the phone is travelling up the M6."

Greco peered over his shoulder. "From the south. It could be our lorry. See if they can match the GPS location to a camera in the area. We need to know if whoever she rang is in a Greysons' lorry."

Speedy was on the phone again. "They've seen it, sir. It's one of Greysons. There are two people in the cab and they are heading north. They have been traced back to Cannock services, where the call was made. We're getting the CCTV from there too."

"In the meantime, don't lose them."

Greco wanted to know just who Ava had rung. He called out to Speedy, "The owner of that phone. It's urgent."

Speedy spent the next few minutes on his phone and computer. "The mobile belongs to a Vasili Pakulski," he told Greco. "We have nothing on him."

"Contact Greysons. Find out if he is an employee there."

If there was a consignment of drugs on board, that could be what Ava was after. Hence the call.

"He's new, sir." Speedy relayed the information as he heard it. "The man has been on a run to Warsaw with a George Potts. It's Pakulski's first trip. Ava Whitton hired him just this week."

"Where does he live?"

"They are checking," Speedy replied. "Ah, Crompton Street, Gorton."

"One of Barton's?"

Speedy nodded. "I'm afraid so, sir."

"Get round there," Greco told Speedy. "Find out about the man. It is probable that Barton has something on him. Get one of his family to talk to you."

"The lorry, sir!" Joel called. "It's pulled off the motorway. It's heading off in the wrong direction. I thought it was going back to base on the Quays. The way it's going will take it into deepest Cheshire."

Greco studied the map and pointed. "Ava Whitton is in that lorry. Look at where they are headed — the site of that pop festival last summer."

* * *

"Can I use your phone?" Ava asked Vasili. "It's possible that the police are monitoring my calls."

He handed it to her without demur. "Where are we?"

"This is where Barton killed my brother, Tomasz. Fitting, don't you think, that Barton should get his here?"

Vasili said nothing. His time with Potts had been bad enough, but this could be worse. He didn't know what Ava had in mind, but he could not sit by and watch her kill Barton in cold blood. The only positive thing was that at least he could communicate with her.

She put the mobile on loudspeaker, nodded at Vasili and tapped in Barton's number.

"Don't speak — listen." Her voice was firm, authoritative. "Your consignment is in my care. If you want it back, you must do as I say."

Several seconds of silence followed. Barton would not be expecting this, Vasili knew. He would be livid at being tricked this way.

Then Barton spoke. "You will follow the plan as arranged, Ava. I have warned you once. Deviate and I will kill you."

"No. The rules are out the window, Barton. I dictate what happens now. You will follow my instructions to the letter. Keep your phone line free. I will call again."

Ava took her rucksack from the floor of the cab. "Thank you, Vasili. You have been a great help to me." She rummaged in the bag and held out a bundle of notes to him. "There is at least ten thousand there. Take it."

They had parked up in a pull-in beside the field. "Just down that path is the main road. A few metres on, there is a village with a bus stop. You can get into Manchester from there. Go. Don't look back, and do not tell anyone what went on today."

Vasili was both surprised and relieved. He could hardly believe that he would be allowed to simply walk away. "Will you be alright? What will you do?"

"Never mind about me. I will be fine. Go, Vasili. Take your family and find somewhere else to live. Do it quickly. Get as far away from Barton's influence as you can. But one more favour." She gave him a rare smile. "Leave me your phone."

Vasili nodded, gathered up his things, and stuffed the money in his bag. He got out of the cab and made for the path.

* * *

Ava watched him go. Once he was out of sight, it was time for phase two.

Ava had written the number on the inside of her arm. She had kept it safe for months. The last thing she'd done before leaving her house was to copy it down. Worried that she might become parted from her belongings, Ava had decided that her own skin was the safest place.

She pressed the keys on Vasili's mobile slowly. This was it. There was no going back. Once she spoke to the man who would answer, she had sealed her fate.

"DI Grant Chambers, please." These few words, spoken in a faltering voice, would change her life forever.

# Chapter 32

"My father is working," Zosia Pakulski told Speedy.

"Do you know when he will be back?"

The young girl shook her head.

"Can I come in? Perhaps speak to your mother?" Speedy asked.

"My mother does not speak much English. And I already told you, my father isn't here. Do you want to speak to Elena? She is my older sister."

Speedy had been kept standing on the front doorstep. It was a miserable part of town, rundown, and even more dismal in the rain. There were slates missing off the roof and the window frames badly needing replacing. The house must be damp and cold. Speedy could not understand how Barton got away with it. He had to have someone on the local council in his pocket — that was how.

The girl who came out looked like her sister, only older and taller.

"You are the police?" Elena said.

Speedy smiled. "Yes. I wanted a word with your father."

"Zosia already told you, he isn't here. Can I help?"

"He changed his job recently. Went to work for Greysons. Do you have any idea why?"

The girl gave Speedy an odd look. "You are really police? This is not some trick to make us slip up?"

"No, I'm definitely police." He handed her his warrant card. "We are investigating three murders as well as drug trafficking," he told the girl.

Elena shook her head. "My father is not mixed up in anything like that! He could not kill, and he hates drugs."

"He may still know things that will help us. Do you know how he got the job with Greysons?"

"Our landlord, Mr Barton, was about to throw us out. We had men at the door," she told him. "I know a young woman. She helps at the community centre. She got him the job. Papa works for Greysons, does as he's told and we get to stay."

"Not so simple, I'm afraid. That young woman you spoke of — is she called Dee?"

Elena nodded.

"She is one of the murder victims. So, you see, Miss Pakulski, the people your father is involved with are killers."

Elena's face went white. "I liked Dee. Without her we would be lost. My father would never hurt anyone. He hates violence."

"When your father gets back, I want to speak to him." Speedy handed her his card. "Don't let me down. His life might depend on it."

\* \* \*

McCabe walked into the incident room. "What are you doing, Stephen?" he asked.

"Tracking a vehicle belonging to Greysons. I think Ava Whitton is on board, her and the latest drug shipment," Greco replied.

"Drop it."

Greco stared at the superintendent in astonishment. He couldn't believe what he'd just heard. The man had to be mistaken. They couldn't drop it, not after all the work they'd put in, not now. They were so close. But McCabe's face was like stone. He meant it alright.

"What is this? I don't understand, sir. We can't just let it go. We are about to close in. The lorry is parked up. It's a gift. We get Ava Whitton, and she will lead us to Barton."

"You are right, Stephen, as usual. And don't think the hard work you and your team have put in is not appreciated. But that particular collar is not for us. The drug squad are taking over. They are moving into position as we speak. DI Chambers will take charge of the case from this point on. Within the last thirty minutes, Ava Whitton rang him and asked for help."

Greco was gobsmacked. He couldn't believe McCabe would simply roll over and allow another branch to steal their case. "The murders, sir. We need to speak to those involved in the drugs case in order to clear those up."

"I said no!" McCabe was red in the face. "Once Chambers has spoken to Whitton, we'll see," he conceded. "But Chambers will be the one to determine whether she can help us or not."

"She knows things. She can really help us." Greco was doing his best not to lose it. Nothing like this had ever happened to him before, and he couldn't believe it was happening now. "You said she asked for help? What sort of help?"

"She is going to give them Barton in exchange for protection, and a deal."

Greco should have guessed. Ava Whitton was a clever woman, and would have had her exit strategy planned and ready to implement. She had offered Chambers something he could not turn down. The chance to get Alex Barton, and clear up the drug trafficking that had long been the bane of his life. "And Chambers is okay with that? The deal I mean. For all we know, the woman is a murderer!" Greco didn't really believe that, but he had no evidence to the contrary.

"I do understand, Stephen, really, I do. You and the team have put in the slog, got so close. But it's out of my hands. The best we can do is see what Chambers turns up, and hope he shares."

Greco had met Chambers, and doubted he would do anything of the sort. Ava and Barton, the two people who were key to his case, were effectively lost to him.

"And if Chambers doesn't share, sir? What do we do then?"

"We wait and see, Stephen."

The problem was, where work was concerned, and this case in particular, Greco was not a patient man. He wanted whoever had killed Craig, Vinny and Dee caught and locked up. He looked around. Where was Grace? For the first time in weeks, he felt the need to talk to her.

* * *

Speedy was back in the incident room. "Pakulski is working for Greysons and in hock to Barton. He was about to get thrown out if he didn't play ball," he said.

"Doesn't matter." Greco's voice was flat. He was sitting at Grace's desk, his face despondent. "We've been told to drop it."

"Why? What the hell's going on? We can't do that! Who wants us to drop it?"

"McCabe."

"Has he lost his head? We've practically got them."

"Watch your mouth, Sergeant," Greco warned him. "That's the super you're talking about. Ava Whitton has offered the drug squad a deal. That effectively rules us out of the picture."

"And we are just going to roll over and accept it?"

"We have no choice, Speedy. We will have to leave them to it for now."

191

"Where is everyone? Do they know about this?"

Greco had been alone in the room for a while. He presumed that the others had gone for something to eat. The day was rolling on. "Joel is following up on the vehicle tracking, I think." Greco looked at the empty desk. "Thankless task now."

"Grace and DI Wells? What are they up to?" Speedy asked.

Greco had no idea.

# Chapter 33

Leah helped Grace to a seat in the waiting area. "They know you're here. It won't be long," she reassured her.

Grace was dabbing her eyes. "I knew this morning that something was wrong. Nothing concrete, just a feeling."

"You've been working hard. It'll just be stress. You need a week off, put your feet up."

Grace gave a half-hearted smile. She knew that Leah was trying to keep her spirits up. But it wasn't working.

"Should I ring Stephen?" Leah said.

"Don't you dare," Grace retorted. "His head is buried in the case. He has no time for anyone or anything else. Not even his baby." As she said these words, Grace choked and burst into tears. She was terrified. She wanted this baby more than anything else. With or without Stephen Greco.

"How about your mother, then?" Leah persisted. "You might need somebody close after you've had the scan."

Grace looked at her. "My mum will be picking Holly up from school soon. No, I'll wait and see what's what first."

A nurse called her name. "Ms Harper? Come with me. We're ready for your scan now."

"Do you want me to come with you?" Leah offered. "If it's bad news, you'll be all on your own in there."

It was kind of her to offer, but Grace and her DI were not particularly close. She shook her head. "I'll be fine," she said without conviction. "But you can wait for me."

Leah nodded.

The nurse helped Grace onto the bed. "What makes you think there is something wrong?" she asked. "You only had your three-month scan earlier in the week. All was well then."

"A feeling," Grace replied. "I woke up this morning and knew it was gone." Her voice was flat. She had rarely felt this sad.

"Gone? Have you been bleeding?"

"No."

The nurse gave her a reassuring smile. "Then the chances are it's just a bout of nerves or something. It says in your notes that you had a tummy upset a couple of days ago."

Grace felt the cold gel on her belly. She turned her head to look at the screen. A few seconds later, the shape of the baby could clearly be seen. For a moment or two, she felt a sweet surge of relief. But the nurse was troubled.

She was pressing the probe on her belly harder, moving right and left. After a few minutes, she gave up. "I'm very sorry, Grace. I'm afraid I can't find a heartbeat," she said at last.

* * *

Leah left the hospital but decided not to return to the station just yet. It would mean answering Greco's questions about where she'd been. She didn't feel up to it.

Leah had never been pregnant. She didn't even know if she wanted kids or not. But losing one, like Grace had, must be an awful experience.

The hospital was keeping Grace in for the time being. Leah had rung Emily Harper and told her. She'd also told her that Greco had no idea what had happened, and for the time being, Grace wanted to keep it that way. Emily Harper had broken down in tears. Leah left Grace in that little room on her own, knowing that at this point her colleague was beyond tears. It was a bad day all round. Time to do something positive, make some headway.

Leah drove to Shona Neville's house. Although it was a school day, the girl was in.

Shona opened the door a crack. "My mum is at work. Don't know if I should let you in. I'm on my own." She had a smirk on her young face. "I'm not up to answering any of your stupid questions. Still feel a bit woozy."

"I am surprised. It's been a day or two, Shona. I thought you'd be well over it by now. How about your friend, Hazel? How is she doing?"

"Why not go and ask her? She didn't take as much of the stuff as me. She's gone back to school." She laughed. "Her mother's not a soft touch like mine."

"Have you thought any more about the lad who gave you the drugs?"

"Yeah, and it's still a blur. I've already told you, I don't know who he is, or where he's from."

Leah could tell she was lying. It showed in the nervous folding and refolding of her arms, and the fact that she couldn't look Leah in the eye.

Leah smiled. "You see, I find it all rather odd. This lad who approached you, he hasn't bothered anyone else. No one else has overdosed. And there aren't any new dealers or drugs being offered out there either."

She stood on the doorstep confronting Shona Neville, who stared up at the sky.

"So? That's not my fault. He must be taking time off. Perhaps he's gone selling somewhere else."

"Come on, Shona. Who was he? Give me a name. This isn't funny. You are holding up an investigation. People have died."

Leah saw another teenager walking up the path. It was Shona's friend, Hazel. Shona came out onto the step. "What's *she* doing here?" the girl shouted.

"The drugs — again!" Shona said scornfully. "I'm sick of it. All this fuss over a bit of gear."

"I've already told you," Leah insisted. "People are dead because of that 'bit of gear,' as you call it."

Hazel threw her school bag onto the step. "My mum is driving me mad about it too. She's given me a right ear bashing. I'll be lucky to get out again any time soon."

"It'll pass," Shona told her.

"No, it won't pass, Shona!" Leah retorted. There was now real anger in her voice. "You are sitting on information that might help us solve three murders!"

"No we're not."

"For God's sake, tell her," Hazel said at last.

Shona pushed her friend. "We can't tell! And you know why."

"Look, if you two are being threatened, I can help." Leah assured them both.

"It's not that," Hazel replied.

"It's my granddad," Shona told a surprised Leah. "We found the drugs in his house. Well hidden, the packets were. A whole shedload of the stuff, all wrapped in plastic. We only tried a bit. We didn't know what to do with it, or how to take it."

"Where does he live, your granddad?" Leah asked.

"On the Lansdowne."

"How old is he?"

"I dunno, somewhere in his seventies."

# Chapter 34

DI Grant Chambers parked his car behind the Greysons lorry and looked around. Ava Whitton was nowhere to be seen. Chambers cursed. The woman had done a runner. He should have guessed. Why hadn't he been more positive when she'd asked about a deal?

The lorry had been left open with the keys in the ignition. On the driver's seat was a letter address to him.

*The drugs are hidden in the second diesel tank. It is two tanks in one with a small reservoir for fuel. Ingenious, and worked perfectly. In all these months customs never found a thing. Not my idea. That one came from Barton. It is a method he has used before.*

*It was my intention to wait for you, but I couldn't take the risk. I will not waste my life in prison. However, this will act as my statement. It will give you everything you need to arrest Barton. I have listed the names and addresses of people in the chain, both here and in Europe, those he relies on to transfer drugs and deal with the tanks.*

*A search of his office and his home will give you the devices, laptop etc., that link to our website on the dark net. We use it to plan shipments, routes etc. I have listed the passwords.*

*Barton converts most of his cash into diamonds. He has a safety deposit box in the main bank in town. He also has houses abroad and uses a number of aliases. His favourite is 'Robert Hilditch.' He has a passport in this name. The box in the bank will be in this name.*

*I suspect that Barton killed my brother. He has a henchman — Archie is the only name I know him by. He is Barton's muscle and a very dangerous man.*

*There is nothing else I can give you. Barton will be suspicious because of my disappearance and the fact that the lorry has not returned to base. Arrest him quickly, or you may lose the chance.*

Chambers re-read the letter. If she was right, they were bound to find sufficient evidence to put Barton away. And she had signed it.

"Time to secure a warrant," he told his team. "Get this crate back to the nick and we'll go after Barton." He nodded at his sergeant. "Find out where he is. Any problems, let me know at once."

\* \* \*

Leah was back at the station. "Jack Neville, seventy-four years old, no record and lives on the Lansdowne," she told Greco and the others. "Shona is his granddaughter, and at last she told me where they got the stuff."

Greco smiled at her. "You did well. We'll go visit the gentleman. See what he has to say for himself." He glanced at Grace's empty chair. "What's the betting he is a member of Marsh's group at the centre, and that Vinny and Craig hid the drugs in his house?"

"Do you think Marsh will know?" Speedy asked.

"We'll talk to him again too."

"Shame about the lorry, sir," Leah said. "Storming in and stealing our case. It's not on."

Greco shrugged. "They are the drug squad, I suppose. It was always their case. Chambers has been on this one for over a year. Ava Whitton was in his sights. Now he has her, and through her, Barton, I hope."

Leah looked unconvinced. "Doesn't help us any though, does it? What about our murders? Do we even get to interview Barton?"

"I reckon so, once Chambers has finished with him. We'll just have to wait our turn." He sighed. "It doesn't sit well, I agree. But there is nothing we can do."

Leah shook her head. "Barton deserves all that's coming to him."

"Does anyone know where Grace has gone?" Greco asked.

Leah held her tongue. She couldn't tell him. Grace had specifically asked her not to.

"Did those girls say where in the house the drugs were hidden?" Speedy called across.

Leah could have kicked herself. She hadn't asked them. The truth was, she'd been so knocked back by what had happened to Grace that she hadn't had her mind in gear.

"Sorry, Speedy, they wouldn't say," she lied. *Weren't asked and didn't volunteer.* "It will be a one-bedroom job. There won't be much to search."

Leah was aware of Greco watching her. Such a basic question, and she hadn't asked it. He'd know something was wrong.

\* \* \*

"Something has gone wrong. The shipment never turned up, and that bitch is still missing." Alex Barton was shoving documents into a briefcase. "Book me a flight for today, alternative identity. It's time to disappear, Archie." He looked at his minder. "You too. Go to the cottage in Ireland. Wait there and I'll be in touch."

"What do you reckon, boss?" Archie said.

"She has gone to the police. If I was in her shoes, that's what I would do. She'll try to broker a deal. And I'll be the prize." He smiled at his henchman. "Won't work, will it? We're a lot cleverer than that. The day Ava Whitton gets the better of me is the day I give up. Book me the flight, then get out. Save yourself."

Barton grabbed his case and left. He was going straight to the airport. He'd pick up his ticket and leave the country. Using his alternative identity and passport, he would go to Spain, disappear for a while. He'd done it before. He knew people there who owed him. They would help.

# Chapter 35

Greco went to see McCabe and told him about the drugs. "I want to search the place," he said. "When we find the heroin, we'll contact Chambers. Turn it over to him."

"You're sure it's the missing stuff from Whitton's house?"

"No, but it's highly likely to be."

McCabe shook his head. "You should leave it to Chambers. He has a specialised team for such matters."

"An elderly man lives in that flat. He is infirm and rarely leaves the house. He's on our patch. He has no record. He's completely unknown to us. I'm sure that he has no idea what he's harbouring at his property. We'll do things calmly and without any fuss. The last thing we want is a drama, and the press alerting."

"Okay, but go careful. The minute you find anything, contact Chambers," McCabe insisted.

Greco would have preferred to take Grace with him. She had the right touch with the elderly. But she was missing again. He decided to ring her, find out what was wrong.

Speedy met him on his return. "Guv, Dominic Hill is still in the cells. Given that Chambers is onto Barton, shall we bail him?"

Greco could see no harm in letting the young man go now. "Okay, but make sure his statement is complete."

Back in the incident room, there was still no sign of Grace. Greco sat down and tapped in her number. There was no answer. Was she unavailable, or avoiding him? He looked round at the others. "Are you lot sure that Grace didn't leave word about where she was going?"

"She said nothing to me," Joel replied.

Leah coughed, hoping he didn't ask her. She would ring Grace herself, she decided. In any case, she wanted to check up on how her colleague was doing.

"I'm going to get a sandwich from the canteen," she told them. "Anyone want anything?"

Greco looked at the clock. It was gone six. He should be going home, but there was still too much to do. "Anything besides chicken or seafood."

\* \* \*

Ava left shortly after writing the letter. She reckoned she had about an hour's start on Chambers. She got the local village bus into Manchester, and from there went to Chorlton Street coach station. A coach was leaving for Folkestone within the hour. She would take it and make her way from there. Not what she'd intended, but it was the safest bet. Ava could not trust Chambers to keep to the bargain. Her phone conversation with him had left her with a nagging doubt. What if there was no deal? What if Barton somehow managed to wriggle off the hook? She would be left high and dry, facing a long prison sentence.

She had money. Most of it was in a bank account in her home town in Poland under her original name. A name unknown to Chambers. But the other detective knew. She had told Greco. It was only a matter of time before they found it. But she could always transfer the money to a safer account online. Ava had a passport in her real name. She would flee. By the time Chambers and Greco pieced it all together, she would be long gone. It was a tempting prospect. They would have Barton, and she would have her freedom.

* * *

"His office reckons he's gone for the day, guv," Chambers' sergeant told him.

"His home?" Chambers said.

"Not there either."

"Get onto the airport. Tell them to hold a Robert Hilditch."

Chambers checked in with his boss and gave him an update. He had to explain that Ava had done a runner. It would not go down well. When it came to court, a person in the witness box was much better than a letter.

"Anything on the search?" he asked.

"All IT equipment has been taken away. We've got someone going to the bank with a warrant."

"Good. All we need now is to get our hands on Barton himself."

"We picked up his minder, that Archie bloke. He was in a café down the road from Barton's office, having his tea. He put up quite a fight, broke Johnson's nose. But he's safely banged up now."

"Ava Whitton? Anything on her?"

"We're doing all the usual, checking with the airport and railways, but there is nothing."

Chambers knew that Ava, too, would have a name and documents she used in such circumstances. Without some stroke of luck, she could be lost to them forever.

* * *

Leah and Joel went with Greco to the flat on the Lansdowne. Jack Neville had no idea what they were going on about. But he did use the centre and did recall Craig and Vinny doing some work for him.

"I needed some stuff taking down to my garage. It's the middle one with the blue door, in that row of them down there." He pointed through the window. "I don't have a car anymore so I keep things I don't need in it. I will have a clear-out one day, I suppose. Our Shona did have a go. She and that mate of hers were going to take some of it to the charity shop, but that never got off the ground."

Greco nodded at Joel. "Go and have a look, will you?"

Jack Neville handed him the key. "I don't understand. What's so special about my garage?"

"We think the lads, Craig and Vinny, hid something in there."

"Hid what? Something valuable?"

"Possibly," Leah told him. "If it's there, it will help us clear up a case we're working on."

Joel was back in minutes. "It's there alright, sir. Neatly packed in cardboard boxes. There is blood on the floor too. It could be where the lads were killed."

"You're sure you knew nothing about this?" Greco asked the elderly man.

"No. They didn't say anything. They put my stuff down there, and that was that," Jack replied.

"When was this?"

"About four weeks ago."

That was too long ago. The heroin had to have been put in the garage within the last week. "Did they come back after that?"

"No, and they are both dead now, so they won't be, will they?"

"Mr Neville, is it possible that you gave them a key to the garage?" Leah asked.

The old man thought for a moment, and then nodded. "Of course. I never realised. I had two keys. I gave Craig one when they were doing the job, but he never gave it me back."

"That's it then, sir," Leah said. "The lads knew exactly where to hide the stuff. They took it from Ava Whitton and stashed it in Jack Neville's garage."

Greco turned to Joel. "Get onto the Duggan, will you? I want a full forensic search of that garage."

# Chapter 36

Greco called the find into the station and left instructions for Chambers to be informed. The team had done enough for one day. It was time to go home. Jack Neville was told that some different policemen would come and collect what they'd found, and not to worry. Having met and spoken to the man, they were well aware that the robbery and murders had nothing to do with him. He was physically incapable for a start.

Greco was exhausted. The day hadn't gone well. Yes, they'd found the heroin. There was no more risk on the streets from that. But Ava Whitton, and more importantly, Barton, were someone else's catch now.

As he turned into his road, he saw Pat watching for him from the front window. She looked upset. Greco groaned. What now?

She started to speak before he was even through the door. "I wanted to ring you but Emily said not to."

"What is the matter? Is Matilda okay?"

"Yes, she's fine, doing some homework."

"She's only six! What sort of school do we send her to?"

"It's a little simple reading, Stephen, nothing heavy. Come in." She stood aside. "This is serious. I need to speak to you."

It sounded ominous. "Has something happened?"

They were walking down the hallway. Pat Greco turned and looked him in the eyes. There were tears streaming down her face.

"Your baby has died, Stephen."

He looked at her for several seconds, wondering if he'd heard right. "What do you mean?" The baby hadn't even been born yet, so how could it die.

"Just that. Earlier today, Grace felt that something was wrong. She went for a scan this afternoon, and there was no heartbeat."

"The baby was fine earlier in the week."

"It's no one's fault," she assured him. "These things happen."

That was why Grace was missing from work. But why hadn't she told him? "She never even rang me." He walked off into his study, and closed the door behind him. The news was bad, the worst. He had to speak to Grace. Try to make it right.

He tapped in her number on his mobile. No answer. She was avoiding him. But why? Because she didn't trust him not to be relieved about the loss, that was why. He understood that, but she was wrong. He wasn't relieved. He felt damned upset. He couldn't leave things like this.

"I'm going out," he called to Pat. "I need to put this right. If I can."

He was soon parked up outside Grace's small terraced house in the backstreets of Oldston. He'd been spotted. Emily Harper was at the door.

"She's not here. They've kept her in, and she doesn't want to see you."

Greco got out of the car and went to speak to her. "Why not? I'm upset about what's happened too."

"Grace doesn't think so. She reckons it'll just be a weight off your mind."

"She's wrong! I might not have realised before, but I do now. I am genuinely sorry about what has happened. And for my behaviour towards Grace."

"That's as may be. You'll have to talk to her. She's in ward seven. Don't tell her I told you."

* * *

Fortunately, the ward was not full of new mums and their babies. Greco was grateful that Grace had been spared that. She was in the far bed by the wall. She spotted him immediately.

"I didn't want you to find out," she said immediately.

"Why not? It was my baby too."

"You don't have to pretend with me anymore, Stephen. Just say it like it is. We had a drunken fumble in Brighton and I got pregnant. It was a mistake, not the foundation for a relationship. I'm not stupid. I know you don't love me. You never have."

He had no ready answer to that. She was right. He said, "I was hoping that when the baby came, once we'd started to be a family, we might grow closer together."

"It doesn't work like that. You tried that with Suzy, didn't you? Or rather she tried it with you. And that didn't work, did it?"

"What do you want from me, Grace?"

"Nothing, Stephen. You're free. Go away. Go and tell Pat that I'm fine and recovering. Tell the team too. I won't be off for long. A week or so and I'll be back at work."

"This isn't how I wanted things to end between us."

"Me neither, but that's how it is. We've lost the baby. The drop of glue that was keeping us together. Now it's gone, there is nothing left."

Greco shook his head. "I feel miserable."

"I don't feel all that jolly myself. But I'll survive, and so will you. Now leave me alone. I need to sleep."

"You're safe in here?" he asked.

"What sort of question is that?"

"You hear such tales, hospitals being full of superbugs, you know the thing."

"The place is fine, Stephen. Don't start. If you're that worried, you'd better get out before you are infected. Now get out of my face!"

Greco had been sitting at the end of her bed. He stood up. Grace didn't want him. She had, in effect, sent him packing. He was a free agent again. For weeks that had been all he'd wanted. But now he felt like an utter failure. He'd let her down. Grace, his aunt, the kids, they had all been looking forward to the new addition. Why hadn't he been able to feel like them?

# Chapter 37

Day 8

Despite a sleepless night, Greco was in early the next morning. He stood staring at the incident board. There were several things still bothering him. The killings and how they were carried out, for a start. Barton would not have drugged his victims first. He'd have had them strung up and tortured until they told the truth. Then he would have finished them off. Whoever killed Craig, Vinny and Dee had operated differently. A copycat, then. But why?

McCabe came into the room and interrupted his thoughts. "Chambers caught up with Barton at the airport. And his right-hand thug was apprehended too. Result, I'd say."

"Has he said anything? Barton?"

"Chambers reckons the villain is worried. They retrieved a fortune in diamonds from a box he kept in a bank in town. All his bank accounts have been frozen. All he has left is whatever he has salted away in off-shore accounts. His drug trafficking operation was administered from a website on the dark net. Chambers has people looking at it. There is no way Barton can wriggle out of this. The evidence is building. This time we really have him."

"The murders?"

"No. Barton told Chambers that he has never met Holt or Riley. Dee Sampson, yes. But not the lads."

"Tomasz Bilinski?"

"We will need a confession to make that stick. As yet, there are no forensics," McCabe admitted.

"What has Ava Whitton said? Got her deal, has she?"

McCabe pulled a face. "No, Stephen. She did a runner. Left a written statement with the information Chambers needed and disappeared. All the stops have been pulled out, but there is no sign of her."

Greco smiled to himself. He couldn't help it. It was totally out of order, but he was glad that Ava had got away. Where the trafficking was concerned, she was as guilty as sin. But she was no killer. He wondered if Chambers knew her real name, if McCabe had told him. A detail like that could easily be overlooked in a complex investigation.

Once McCabe had left, he checked the system. Forces across the country had been told to look out for her. But the person they were looking for was Ava Whitton, not Bilinski. Right or wrong, he wouldn't tell them just yet.

"Apparently Barton is about to cough," was Speedy's opener that morning. "That should have been ours." He sat down and swung his long legs under the desk. "What about the bird? What's she had to say for herself?"

He meant Ava. "I'm not sure." Greco was deliberately vague. "Grace has lost the baby," he told him, changing the subject. "She won't be in."

This silenced Speedy. Within a few minutes, Joel and Leah came in.

Greco challenged Leah. "You took Grace to hospital yesterday. You were missing, as I recall. You knew what had happened. You might have told me."

"Grace told me not to, sir," Leah replied. "It was her choice, not mine."

"Well, it's done now. Grace will have some time off. We'll have to soldier on without her." He didn't say more. He didn't want to. The details of his private life were not a topic for the incident room.

Leah smiled at him. "I'll arrange some flowers. From all of us."

Greco nodded. "That's a nice idea. I'll give you some money."

The room was quiet. Greco had asked them to look through the statements and the reports from the Duggan again. He wanted to ensure they hadn't missed anything.

"It's the names written across their chests — why do that? It is definitely something Barton would not do."

"We've ruled out Dominic Hill. And if we don't think it was Barton, who does that leave, sir?" Leah asked.

Greco sighed. "Graham Clovelly, Dave Holt, Marsh, half the youngsters that use the centre. We need to look again."

"We have statements from all of them, alibis as well. We have ruled those names out already," Speedy reminded him.

"Nevertheless, there is something we've missed, that we're not seeing."

Speedy shrugged. "Barton. Has to be. He wanted his drugs back. It's simple enough."

"No, it isn't. He would not leave them like that." Greco shook his head.

"They had marker on their chests. So what?" Leah added.

"Leah, they were drugged too," Greco reminded her. "Barton does not anaesthetise his victims before he beats them to a pulp. He'd get nothing from them for a start."

Greco looked at the board again. "That has been bothering me for days."

"What, sir?" asked Leah.

"The drugging of the victims. Whoever killed them wasn't after information. He couldn't have been. He simply wanted to make it look like a Barton execution."

Speedy had his head down, the Duggan reports spread out on his desk. "If we go with that, where does it leave us?"

"The killer murdered the lads so he could keep the heroin for himself. He doesn't need information about what they've done with it because he already knows," Greco said. "If the killer is not one of the names we are already familiar with, then he was an unknown party in all this."

"That buggers up our investigation, sir. We've gone with the premise that only Craig and Vinny knew."

"Someone else had to be involved, Speedy. All we have to do now is find out who."

Speedy looked at him. "You're talking about a third party who wanted to keep the lot for himself? Did for Craig and Vinny, and has been lying low since?"

Greco nodded.

"Perhaps we should look again at the community centre," Speedy suggested. "With luck, whoever that third party is won't yet know that the drugs have been found."

Greco got to his feet. "My money is on Callum Riley."

"The quiet twin? Why him?" Speedy asked.

"He is all we are left with."

\* \* \*

Clovelly didn't look too pleased to see the detectives. "Who rang you? It's nothing. I can deal with it myself."

A strange greeting, Greco thought. "No one. What's happened?"

"A bit of a ruck between Callum and Josh over there. But it's under control now. I've calmed them down."

"What are they fighting about?" asked Speedy.

"I need to rearrange the pool team. We've a match tonight. I've lost Craig and Vinny, remember. Callum wants the chance, but Josh has always been a much better player."

Greco waited, then asked, "Does Callum usually lose his cool? It's not the impression his mother gave us."

"He's upset, grieving for his brother. He won't have meant anything by it, just lost it in a fit of temper. This is an emotional time for the lad."

"Tell us what he did, Graham," asked Speedy.

"Callum went for Josh. Took his pool cue and would have lamped him with it if I hadn't grabbed it first. Not like Callum at all. He's been a lot edgier since Craig."

That was reasonable enough. What happened was bound to have upset the lad. "Can I have a word with them?" Greco asked.

Clovelly nodded. "But don't go on about the row. Like I said, I'll deal with it."

Clovelly gathered the lads together. Callum Riley stood apart from the others, a scowl on his face.

"The haul of drugs stolen by Craig and Vinny has been found and is now safe in our hands." Greco looked around at the faces, gauging reactions. But no one appeared particularly interested, or asked any questions about the find. The revelation was a non-event as far as they were concerned.

Clovelly smiled. "I for one am pleased about that. If that stuff had hit the streets, we would have had one huge problem."

"You know where Craig was, then? When he got himself killed?"

The question came from Callum Riley.

"We will know the answer to that soon," Greco replied. This wasn't the place to discuss it. Callum no doubt had his reasons for wanting to know exactly what happened to his brother, but the other lads didn't need it thrusting down their throats.

"Is it somewhere nearby?"

He was Craig's twin, it was natural for him to be curious. But there was something about the lad's demeanour that bothered Greco. He looked shifty. It was more than just having got into a fight. He was nervous, scared even. His eyes constantly darted from one detective to the other.

"Were you there, Callum?"

The question appeared to have stunned the lad. Greco wasn't even sure why he'd asked it. If he didn't know his methods better, he'd have put it down to gut instinct.

"No! I was here, you know that." He backed away slightly. "I can't believe you are still asking me that. I have a cast-iron alibi. I had nothing to do with Craig's death."

He spoke with conviction. So why was Greco so suspicious? Of all the youngsters who came here, Callum was the one Craig would have trusted. Nonetheless, Greco had thought all along that the lad must know more than he was saying. But why would he not tell them?

"Okay, thank you for your time." Greco told the group. The youngsters dispersed and he turned to Speedy. "Do we have Callum Riley's fingerprints?"

"I'm not sure, sir," he replied. "I'll check with the Duggan. He was never questioned formally. The prints on the jewellery taken from Ava Whitton's house were hers, plus Craig and Vinny's. There were no others. And his alibi was fine. If fingerprints were taken, it'll have been for elimination purposes."

Greco frowned. "Those packets containing the heroin. Tell the Duggan to rush the prints through on those, will you?"

Suddenly there was a crash. Callum Riley had smashed his cue down on the pool table, breaking it in two, and was threatening Josh with the thicker half.

Speedy darted forward. "Stop that! What's your problem?" He grabbed Callum by the arm and shook him. "You need to calm down, pal. If you hit him, you'll be in a heap of trouble."

Callum wriggled free. "Get lost, copper. Leave me be."

Clovelly hurried towards them. "I don't know what's got into him. He is never like this. Callum! You'd better go home. Your mother needs help with the funeral arrangements. And don't forget her prescription." He turned to Greco. "You don't need him, do you?"

Greco shook his head.

"He was on his way to the chemists when he got sidetracked and ended up here. Desperate to get into the team, he is. But I have to say, his game has improved. He must have been practising."

"Is his mother ill?"

"She's living on her nerves at the moment. Needs something to help her sleep I shouldn't wonder. Then there are her daily injections to organise."

"Can I take this?" Greco picked up the half cue that Callum had brandished at Josh. "Who else has used it?"

"No one. Callum bought it new just yesterday."

Back in the car, Greco put the broken cue into a plastic bag. "The Duggan," he told Speedy.

Speedy turned the car. "What's your thinking, guv?"

"I'm thinking young Callum is suddenly a lot edgier than he was. There is something on his mind, and I want to know what. Also his mother has daily injections. What's the betting she's diabetic and those injections are insulin?"

"You think he's our killer?"

"Despite what the evidence is telling us, there is something not right there." Greco phoned Joel and asked him to check the woman's medical history.

* * *

"What am I looking for?" Roxy Atkins asked.

"Prints, fresh ones. I want to know if they are a match for any on those plastic bags you're looking at," Greco said.

"Ah, the stash of heroin." She smiled. "I've had a DI Chambers on the phone asking about that. I was a little vague with him, but I'll have to come clean soon."

"Get us the prints first, Roxy, and then he can have the lot," Greco told her.

"Go and get a cup of tea, the both of you. I'll rush this through."

Greco didn't feel like swigging tea. He wasn't sure what Roxy's tests would throw up, but despite catching Barton, they were still desperate for that break.

Speedy put two mugs on the table. "No sugar in yours. Want a bite to eat?"

Greco shook his head. "A result, that's all I want. The killer of those two lads."

"Where d'you reckon the posh bird has gone?"

"Ava? She can look out for herself. She will have a bolthole somewhere. I doubt we'll hear from her again."

"She had a driver, a Polish chap. I went to his house yesterday. He was coerced into working for Barton and driving for Greysons. Barton would have thrown his family on the streets if he hadn't done what he was told."

"We will speak to him. But he is going to be of more use to Chambers. He will have seen Barton's operation first hand."

"Have you considered Martin Greyson's part in all this?" Speedy asked.

"Only that Ava ran rings around him. She was the one who organised the drug runs. Greyson is now Chambers' problem, not ours."

Speedy looked at him. "What will you do about Grace? Are you still a couple, or what?"

Trust Speedy. Straight to the point, no matter how painful. "I don't know. That will be up to Grace. But I don't think I'm top of her favourites list at the moment."

"Shame about the baby. We're all sorry, sir."

"I just want to see an end to this case, and for things to get back to normal."

Just then a voice called out. "Stephen! I've done your tests. And, you'll be pleased to know, I have found a match for the prints on the broken cue."

Greco smiled at her. "I knew it. The plastic packets the heroin was wrapped in?"

"Yes."

Greco looked at Speedy. "Callum Riley, had to be. My instinct was right. Let's go and pick him up. We now have the proof we need."

Roxy looked puzzled. "Who?"

"Callum Riley, the owner of those prints," Greco repeated.

"I'm afraid not, Stephen. I have no idea what you had in mind, but the prints on that cue belong to *Craig* Riley."

# Epilogue

"That was a real turn-up. None of us saw that one coming." Speedy grinned. "But at least we've got it sorted at last."

"Murdered his own twin? Then took his identity?" Leah sounded incredulous.

"His twin, Vinny, and then Dee," Greco said. "We came within a whisper of missing it too. If it hadn't been for that visit to the centre this morning, we'd have been none the wiser."

"You did suspect Callum, sir," Speedy reminded him.

Greco shook his head. "But I didn't for one minute suspect that Craig had taken his brother's identity. I suspected the real Callum."

Leah smiled. "Craig had everyone fooled. But what about his mother? Didn't she notice?"

"Different clothes, a change of attitude and there you are. And she's got dodgy eyesight," Speedy reminded them. "Couldn't keep the pretence going though, could he? Craig has a temper and in the end, it gave him away. His mother said he had a short fuse."

"Is it true that their DNA is the same, sir?" Joel asked.

"Yes, but if you ask Professor Batho, I'm sure he'll know about some complex method of determining minute differences. In the end, for our purposes, it was all down to fingerprints."

"Has he coughed yet?" Speedy asked.

"More or less, but we'll interview him again shortly. He realises that lying to us is pointless. I have told him we have evidence that he is, in fact, Craig Riley and not Callum."

"I wonder how long he'd been planning this little lot for?"

"We'll be sure to ask him, Speedy."

Greco led the way down the corridor to the interview room. Craig Riley was sat on a chair, his hands in his jeans pockets.

"This is my brief," he said with a smile. "Never had one before."

Greco ignored the comment. "I'd like you tell us exactly what happened that night, Craig," Greco began. "Take your time, start at the beginning."

He pulled a face. "You already know. What are you making me go through it all again for? I don't like thinking about it, upsets me." He looked at them. "I'm not proud of what I did. It just sort of happened."

"That isn't true. You must have planned it. You were prepared, the syringes, the drugs. What you did was no spur of the moment act," Greco said.

"We arranged to meet that night after me and Vinny stole the drugs. We had sorted a hiding place in an old mill with Dom. He wanted his payoff. It was him who gave us the tip-off about the stuff being at the bird's place. But I wasn't happy. I spoke to Vinny about Dom's share. We'd taken all the risks. I told him I thought we were giving him too much. We had a bit of a ruck over that one. Too fair-minded for his own good was Vinny."

"When you took the drugs from the house in Handforth, what did you do with them?" Greco asked.

"Me and Vinny split the haul and kept it with us. We dumped it at the old bloke's later that night."

Speedy asked. "What was Callum doing there?"

"I tried to persuade Vinny to cut Dom out of the deal. I wanted us to keep the gear, sell it ourselves. Vinny was dead set against that. He wanted to go with the original plan to blackmail the bird into giving us money to get it back. I didn't want to do that. I tricked Vinny into going to the old bloke's first. Said I wanted something I'd stashed there."

"What did you do next?" Greco asked.

"Fair enough — I had made plans. If Vinny had gone along with what I wanted, we would've got rid of Dom and everything would've been fine. But he didn't. And then our Callum stuck his oar in. I was getting ready to meet up with Vinny when Callum found the bag I'd put my half of the stuff in. He was angry. Threatened to tell you lot. I couldn't have that. I said I'd cut him in. All he had to do was come with me that night." He hung his head and went silent for a few moments. "I didn't want to kill them, but I had no choice. They wouldn't listen to me. I had to do something. I couldn't let the chance of getting all that money slip through my fingers. Callum was shouting at Vinny. Telling him what a moron he was for hanging around with me. I lost it. I stuck both of them with a syringe full of ketamine. It didn't take long before they were both out of it. The rest you know."

"Why the violence on the bodies?" Speedy asked.

"Barton, that's his trademark, particularly the finger thing. Dom told me. I thought it would send you his way."

"And the names written on their chests?" Greco asked.

Craig Riley smiled. "Had to make sure you blamed the right twin."

"Dee? Why her?"

"She knew stuff. Dee guessed about us stealing from the old folk. You brought her here, spoke to her. Sooner or later, she would have said the wrong thing. I couldn't risk that."

* * *

"He made it all sound so easy," Speedy said. "He killed the pair of them in cold blood."

They were back in the incident room. Greco and Speedy had related the interview details to rest of the team.

Superintendent McCabe entered the room with a big smile on his face. "Congratulations, Stephen, to you and the team. You got there in the end. Never doubted you would."

"Thank you, sir."

"Sorry to hear about DC Harper. She is going to be alright, isn't she?"

"I'm sure she'll be fine," Greco replied. Truthfully, he had no idea. He had tried to phone her, but she'd refused to speak to him.

"No doubt, she will be off sick for a while. We will have to look at the caseload. Speaking of which, can I have a private word?"

Greco took the super into his office and shut the door behind them. The DCI presumed that it must have something to do with Grace and their relationship. This was where he got the telling-off.

"I realise you are short-handed. But something has come up. I would allocate the case to another team, but this has the potential to be big."

Another case, and so soon. Greco had been hoping for a couple of days' down time, at least. On the other hand, perhaps he should be flattered that McCabe still trusted him, given recent history.

"The case requires an SIO with a sensitive touch. I have put you forward, Stephen."

## THE END

Thank you for reading this book. If you enjoyed it please leave feedback on Amazon, and if there is anything we missed or you have a question about then please get in touch. The author and publishing team appreciate your feedback and time reading this book.

Our email is office@joffebooks.com

www.joffebooks.com

ALSO BY HELEN H. DURRANT

**CALLADINE & BAYLISS**
Book 1: DEAD WRONG
Book 2: DEAD SILENT
Book 3: DEAD LIST
Book 4: DEAD LOST
Book 5: DEAD & BURIED
Book 6: DEAD NASTY
Book 7: DEAD JEALOUS

**THE DCI GRECO BOOKS**
Book 1: DARK MURDER
Book 2: DARK HOUSES
Book 3: DARK TRADE
Book4: DARK ANGEL

**DI MATT BRINDLE**
HIS THIRD VICTIM

37652858R00141

Made in the USA
San Bernardino, CA
01 June 2019